The WAR Council

University Chronicles Book 1

Ann Shepphird

The WAR Council

University Chronicles Book 1

4 Horsemen
Publications, Inc.

The War Council
University Chronicles Book 1
Copyright © 2021 Ann Shepphird. All rights reserved.

4 Horsemen
Publications, Inc.

4 Horsemen Publications, Inc.
1497 Main St. Suite 169
Dunedin, FL 34698
4horsemenpublications.com
info@4horsemenpublications.com

Typesetting by Michelle Cline
Editor JM Paquette

Library of Congress Control Number: 2021941364

Paperback ISBN-13: 978-1-64450-258-7
Audiobook ISBN-13: 978-1-64450-253-2
Ebook ISBN-13: 978-1-64450-257-0

For the friends and family that make up my
own personal war council.
Thank you for all your love and support.

Chapter One
MAGGIE

O kay. Let's get one thing straight—it's not that I feel that I have to justify myself. Because I don't. I just want you to understand how this all came about. Because, really, it was a logical decision. Very logical.

We're talking about love here. Now many may argue that love is inherently illogical. "Sweet mystery of love" and all that crap. But that doesn't necessarily mean that we have to be illogical when it comes to our relationships. There are just so many signs out there that people are straining for some sort of logic. They turn to self-help books, therapists, relationship blogs, even Goop, for god's sake. But, let's face it—they're all inherently impersonal.

So, we turn to our friends. How many hours have we spent listening to our friends' relationship woes? How many hours have we spent pouring our hearts out to our friends about our own relationships? Hours. Many many hours.

Many many friends. And yet, how good is the advice? I mean, really? How many times have you done something incredibly stupid just because a friend advised it? I have. I will admit it. Sometimes love makes us so crazy that we don't know how to act—and so we act stupidly. That's just my point.

But what if there was a way to face love logically? Armed with a plan that had at least a modicum of logic and reason? See, that's the real problem. When we fall in love, we lose all sense of logic and reason. So where should we turn to receive advice that is logical and reasonable? To other lovesick puppies? Or to a team of experts whose sole purpose it is to be logical and reasonable when you're not capable of either? To a therapist? Or to a group of specialists who don't just listen to your problems but become actively involved in them with you? A professional council of experts who are paid to be on your side. I'm talking about a business. A desperately needed service. Are you following me here?

This idea, simple as it may seem, did not come about immediately. It evolved. But, once again, it just seemed so right.

Maybe it would help to give you a little background. I suppose my background should come first. Not that I run around talking about myself all the time. I don't. Really. But it might clarify how I came to this idea. I was 30. There is something about turning 30 that forces a re-examination of one's life. I mean, it's the end of an era, right? Not that I really enjoyed my 20s. Most of it was the shits. Constantly growing, constantly changing, constantly figuring out what the hell I wanted to do with my life. I'm still not sure I know. Do we ever know? But I had done a lot of examining. And most of my non-career examining had to do with relationships. It started the first time I fell in love.

I fell in love—real love, real down-to-the-cellular-level love—for the first time somewhat later than most, I suppose. I was 25. Like I said, a little late. Maybe it's better to go through it in your teens when your hormones make you an idiot anyway. Maybe it's not. It was nice to be a little formed before the big fall because, let's face it, love fucks us up majorly. We search for it so desperately, and yet when it hits—wow. I don't think we're ready.

So anyway, I was 25 and swept off my feet. God, I hate that expression. Like I'm some Cinderella obsessive or something. I'm not. Still, the phrase fits. I'm not sure we ever feel the same as we do with that first love. It was amazing. Overwhelming. Liberating, really. I changed—or, at least, I felt like I changed. I began to believe in myself. I felt beautiful, sexy, intelligent—like I could do anything. Everything changed. Those feelings of being beautiful, sexy, and intelligent translated to how I carried myself, and it was like the world responded. I even got off my butt, went back to my graduate program, and got my Ph.D.

The first year with Bill... Yeah, I know. Bill. Sucks, doesn't it? But consider the alternatives: William, Willie, Billy—they all suck. Anyway, that first year was fabulous. Well, not always fabulous. Every month or so I would get a speech about how he wasn't ready for marriage. Like I was? This kind of pissed me off. I was 25 years old—we were both 25—so who said I wanted to marry him? I do think it is rather egotistical—sexist, even—of men to think every woman wants to trap a man into marriage.

That's why this idea of mine is really NOT gender specific. But we'll get into that later.

Really, though, the first year was great. Mostly because I was really good at giving Bill space when he needed it. It was kind of natural. I've always been kind of a space nut myself. So, whenever I got the speech about marriage and space and whatever, I said, "Fine. Take all the space you want," and he didn't want the space, and everything was fine.

The problems started when Bill was about to get his degree. He was finishing his master's in journalism, and I kind of knew he wouldn't stay in Berkeley after he graduated, but I didn't want to think about it. Unfortunately, he thought about it a lot. That was another speech I got. He was always saying how special we were together and how much he loved me, but that it couldn't last because he was going to leave soon. He had big plans for his life, and he wasn't going to let a little thing like love get in his way. I was okay with it. Sure. And, of course, I will admit that I was warned. That didn't mean it wasn't a shock when he actually left.

Bill got a job at a wire service in Tokyo, and I was destroyed. The thing is it's not as if I wouldn't have dropped everything to go with him. I would have. See, that's how sick love makes us. I would have left everything I had built to follow him. But he didn't want me. He said he loved me, but he had to do this on his own. I said I understood but really I didn't.

I guess I just see things in very simple terms. Or I used to. I just think that if two people love each other, they should be together. Bill didn't think it was that easy. His parents had divorced when he was young, and he thought that love led to marriage, which led to fights, which led to divorce. He didn't want anything holding him back in his life, and unfortunately, he saw me as holding him back. More male ego if you ask me. Again, I never said that I wanted to marry him and strap him down with kids and a Volvo. I have never been the white picket-fence type. I just wanted to be with him. Simple. But, not for him. So, we were not to be. This is when I did those really stupid and embarrassing things. But we don't need to go into them here, do we?

Like I said, I was destroyed. I didn't understand how someone could say they loved me more than anything else in the world, that we were special, that we had everything in common—and then leave. I did a lot of growing up. I sure wonder how teenagers get over a first love when I was heartbroken at 28 while finishing my dissertation. Suddenly, I wasn't so sure that I was beautiful, sexy, or intelligent. I thought he made me those things, and without him, I was nothing. I know—dumb, huh?

It was then that I started my analysis of relationships. And the phone calls began. And the emails and texts. My friends became sick of me. So, I moved to new friends. Then a therapist. I had to get things straight in my mind. How could this have happened? What did I do? What could I have done? More phone calls. More emails. More texts. But the answer was always the same. Nothing. I did nothing. I could do nothing.

It was then I realized how much timing has to do with relationships. Bill didn't leave because of me. He left because of him. He was selfish. He never even considered my feelings. I had nothing to do with his decision or his life. I then realized I could be beautiful, sexy, and intelligent without him. Fuck him. I started to wonder how I could have given him so much power. How could someone place her entire self-esteem in the hands of another person? Especially the egotistical male creature?

Sorry. I know I said that this would not be gender specific. But, really, Bill was thinking about himself, and I was thinking about Bill and what I thought he made me. I gave him a lot of power. And, to his credit, he never asked for that power.

It was then that I realized that this is what relationships are all about. Power. Who has it. And
who has given it up.

If relationships are about power, then it
stands to reason that the more people we have
on our side, the better, right? That's why we call
our friends. We explain our side. They agree. We
feel better. We have ammunition.

Aha. Power. Ammunition. Sounds like a battle,
right? Right. Battle of the sexes. All's fair in love
and war. Clichés, yes, but there's a reason they're
clichés. So instead of having a bunch of friends
on our side, what if we could have experts on
our side? A "War Council," so to speak? What if
our ammunition came from seasoned specialists
who analyzed our relationship and sent us back
out with strategies designed for success? What
if these experts went further and became part
of the scenario? You know, like the team from
"Mission: Impossible." Huh? Still with me?

It was then that I noticed the obsession so
many people have with marriage. As a goal.
Not finding somebody to spend your life with,
to love, to be your best friend—no, to marry. To
experience the convention of marriage. I mean,
look at the success of shows like "The Bachelor"
and "The Bachelorette." I began to notice how
many weddings I attended where the people
didn't seem to love each other as much as the
show they were putting on. God, how many
bridal showers—an archaic and sickening convention if ever there was one—have I attended

where all the women did was go gah-gah over the rocks on their fingers while bitching about their husbands?

I noticed how many of the self-help books and blogs and conferences had to do with coercing someone into marriage. One even goes so far as to tell women not to sleep with the man until he's proposed. Heck, even my grandmother used to say you don't buy a shoe until you've tried it on (and we won't even talk about what happens in those Fantasy Rooms on "The Bachelor"). How many times do even astrology columns mention things like "attention revolves around marital status"? I'll tell you: Lots.

Okay. So. We know it's an obsession. We know people would like more ammunition in the power struggle in their relationships, and that for most, the final goal is marriage. Well, there you have it: a War Council whose aim is to coerce a partner into the ultimate commitment. The business opportunities seemed boundless. We could provide a necessary service. Those stupid self-help books were making a fortune. And this was SO much better.

Cynical, yes. But, hey, these are cynical times.

The first time I tried the idea out on "the public," so to speak, was at one of Kathy's dinner parties. Kathy is my best friend—if those are still around. We have known each other for years.

Got our doctorates at UC Berkeley together, although hers is in psychology and mine's organizational communications. Kathy is one of those people who has seemingly sailed through life. I don't know how she does it. Always even keel, always thinks the best of people, just kind of floats. I'd use the word mellow if I didn't hate it so much.

Naturally, we are total opposites. I can be somewhat mercurial. And, okay, I'll admit that I can make things more dramatic than they need to be. Kathy is pretty good at keeping me semi-stable—one of those friends who didn't give up on me during the whole post-Bill thing.

Kathy, naturally, is married to her college sweetheart Brian. They met in Psych 10, discovered they had everything in common, and haven't been apart since. It's enough to make you want to vomit. They have two kids (naturally). A boy and a girl (naturally). I feel a little sorry for the kids, though. You would think having two psychologists for parents would be enough to send someone over the edge. But they seem okay.

So, anyway, Kathy loves to throw dinner parties. Some sort of nesting instinct or something. I don't know. They've got one of those great old Victorians in San Francisco (bought for a song at the right time and fixed up themselves, naturally) and love to have people over. They throw great dinner parties. Always seem to find the most fascinating people to invite. And they usually include me, which is nice. Nurturing types, you know.

This particular dinner party had a lot of close friends. People I had known for years at UC Berkeley.

I had been playing with this War Council idea for weeks and, after a few glasses of wine, decided to try it out on this crowd. They didn't treat it as seriously as I might've liked. Randy, a film scholar, started espousing romantic lines from some 1940s Bette Davis classic, while Monique, a women's studies professor, talked about love as evidence of the patriarchal society's attempts to put women in their "place." I always loved listening to Monique talk like that because she's one of those tall drop-dead gorgeous women who have men, women—everybody, really—eating out of her hand. Not that women's studies professors can't be stunners. I get that. But let's just say that with her mane of blond hair and tendency to wear deep red lipstick, the first impression she gives off is pretty much the opposite of everything that comes out of her mouth. And, yes, again, I get it. That's the point. But, let's be honest: It was a bit of a dichotomy.

Anyway, others piped in with their viewpoints and made some jokes, but then they moved on to another topic. I'll admit I wanted more, but to pressure them seemed futile. As I watched them all talk, I started to scan the table, thinking about

what each had said and stood for in this game—
this war game—of love.

Across from me sat Kathy. Happily married.
Counsels students on campus. Next to her was
Nick, a friend of Brian's. I didn't know much
about him. But then there was Hallie, a political
science professor and one of the most compet-
itive people I knew. Randy, her husband—a film
archivist and true romantic—sat next to her. Then
there was Mike, the new Cal rugby coach. And
Monique. Brian sat next to me.

As I stared at them, a light bulb went off.
This group of people would be perfect. Each
could represent a different "expert" for the
War Council. I didn't see Nick or Brian fitting in.
Brian is a research psychologist more interested
in studying lab rats and their reaction to light
as it relates to seasonal affective disorder than
love and relationships, while Nick said something about studying French literature so neither of them had any practical expertise for the
War Council.

But the others did. The others did! Here I was
playing with this idea of a War Council filled with
experts providing ammunition for relationship
power struggles and who should I see sitting
before me (in my admittedly somewhat-tipsy
state) but the very experts I was seeking!

I mean, think about it. Kathy could be the
interpersonal communications expert. She
knows every psychological nuance in the book,

every non-verbal technique, plus she's warm, nurturing, mothering. Perfect.

Hallie could be the tactical expert. The woman teaches historical war strategies for god's sake. Perfect.

Her husband Randy could be the romance expert. Warm, lovable—and he knows every romantic scenario that has ever been filmed. Perfect.

Mike, please, Mike was perfect for the masculinity expert. The man coaches rugby. Need I say more?

And Monique. It wouldn't work without Monique. Gotta have the feminist tactician to counteract Mike's machismo.

They were all perfect for what I had in mind.

So, there I was. And, again, I'm not trying to justify myself, but I had an idea that was damn solid. And I had the personnel to make it happen. What lay before me was the task of putting the two of them together. It wasn't going to be easy.

Chapter Two
CINDY

I couldn't believe the little shit had done it to me again. There I was, sitting at Café Strada, and Biff was nowhere to be seen. I looked at my watch. Almost 2:30. I knew he had a class at three. His sociology class. So, he wasn't coming. Again. What a little fuckface poophead. I hated him. If he wasn't so cute, it really would've been over right then. Over. Shit, this was embarrassing.

Café Strada is one of those places where everybody is with somebody. It's right across from the UC Berkeley campus so students go there between classes to study or hang out or just to be seen. I was being seen. By myself. The only one alone at Café Strada.

I looked around the café. Nope. Didn't know a soul. I couldn't believe none of my sorority sisters were there. I was totally alone. Great for my image. Just great. Shit. I really did hate the bastard.

I looked to my right. There was a teaching assistant running his discussion section outside. Boy, was he cute. I couldn't remember his name, but I had had his discussion section when I took anthro. I never understood a single word that came out of his mouth, but he always looked SO cute saying them. I remembered how he always wore the same clothes week after week. It made me wonder why grad students always seemed to dress so poorly. This one wore a tweed blazer and jeans. Same tweed blazer. Same jeans. The jeans hung great, though, and he had the cutest little buns. We all thought so. I remembered sitting in his class with Bunny and Jane just staring at those buns every time he turned to write on the board. They were amazing.

Uh oh. He looked over at me. Probably noticed I was alone. Probably thought "that poor twit can't even find someone to sit with at Strada." Shit.

To my left was a group of—it looked like Italians—laughing and talking (and gesturing) in Italian and drinking their macchiatos. They looked like they were having so much fun. Italian boys are such babes. Babe-alicious, Jane always says. The one sitting on the bench with the brown eyes and the brown shoulder-length hair was a real doll. Oooh. Total babe. He looked really thoughtful, too. Like he was thinking about important issues and world events. He'd probably never give me the time of day. At least Biff treated me like I was important. When he wasn't standing me up. Shit.

I had just finished my second cappuccino of the afternoon, and my head was spinning. I should really never drink caffeine, let alone two cappuccinos. It was three o'clock now. Biff was in class. It would be at least an hour before I could happen to pass by his classroom and run into him. Why was he such a fuckface? He hadn't always been like this. I remembered the first time we went out. It was SO great.

Biff and I met through a set-up. I was in this sorority that was, like, the best sorority on campus. I felt really lucky to be in it. We had three big parties every year. Date parties. Had to have a date. I had never been very good at asking guys out. I dunno. I was just not very comfortable about it, you know? I'm not very comfortable around boys in general. I come from an all-girl family, and in high school, we always just did things in groups. That's why the sorority was so great. I had SO many friends and they were going to be my best buds for life. But boys... they always seemed like a species from another planet. Regular old exchanges—which are, like, casual parties where a fraternity comes over and we all hang out—were okay because I could talk to boys with my best bud girl friends at my side.

15

Bunny, especially, was good to have at my side. She was SO funny. People always liked Bunny right away. Boys REALLY liked Bunny. It seemed so easy for her to talk to them, too. I liked that she took me along a lot when she was going out. Bunny was the one who set me up with Biff.

The party was a pledge-active. That's where the pledges throw a party for us actives. They had come up with this really clever theme, too. It was "come as your favorite drink." I liked that. Bunny was going as a Blue Nun, which is like this wine brand that was big in her mom's day. So funny and retro, right? Her current boyfriend, Clay, was going as Christian Brothers, which I guess is a brandy, but they thought it was cool because they were, like, going as a nun and a monk.

I had decided to play it safe and go as Scotch on the rocks. I had this kilt that was my grand-mother's, and I would carry around some rocks. Not too exciting, but it would do. I had no idea what Biff would go as. I didn't even know what he would look like. Some of the guys I'd been set up with were real nimrods. Anyway, Biff was a friend of Clay's from the frat so that would make it more comfortable.

Bunny wasn't at the house when Biff came to pick me up. She was over at Clay's, and they would meet us there. Bummer. I would have felt better if she were there. I was so totally freaked. I paced my room. I felt really stupid in the kilt and carrying the rocks. I wanted to die. I heard the doorbell ring from my room, and Debbie called up that my date had arrived. I walked downstairs and looked toward the front room. There he was. And wow, what a sight.

Biff was wearing a Budweiser suit. Like, a suit covered with Budweiser logos. Like they were part of the fabric. It was SO rad. I couldn't believe it. And I couldn't believe Biff. He was super gorgeous. I couldn't believe how I had lucked out after all the losers I'd been stuck with. Biff had these green eyes that just burned right through me and this sandy-colored hair that waved just a little. He was tall and slender and, well, just perfect.

"Hey, baby, don't you look a sight."

And, oh, the words that came from Biff's mouth. Wondrous words. He was just wonderful. And he seemed to think I was okay. How cool was that? He said that Clay had told him that I was pretty cool, and he thought Clay was pretty cool so it had to be true. See what I mean? Just wow.

We got to his car, and it was a convertible bug. Total coolness. Biff told me he wanted to make one stop before we went to the party. He took me up to the top of the Berkeley hills where there was this lookout point. The sun was about to set behind San Francisco, and it was just beautiful. Biff pulled out a bottle of champagne and a couple of glasses, and we sat and watched the sun set. It was so hyper-romantic that I thought I was gonna die.

And we talked. Mostly about our childhoods. Biff was from Hillsborough. His real name was Robert Billingsley V. Whoosh. With a name like that, I could see why he would want to be called Biff. He didn't look like a "fifth" of anything. He just looked cute. I told him about growing up in Santa Rosa. How boring it was. How I couldn't wait to come to the city and start my life. How I loved Cal and the sorority and my classes and my friends and Café Strada. He was so easy to talk to that I just kept talking and talking and talking.

Finally, though, we had to go to the party. The party was a hoot, mostly because of Biff. He was just so funny. Biff and Clay could sing all these songs. Mostly they were dirty and some of the girls—the ones taking women's studies— kept saying they were sexist and misogynist, but I thought they were funny. And he looked SO cute singing them. It was also fun to see what everybody was wearing. Some of the costumes were pretty neat—there was a Blue Hawaiian, Cold Duck, Dr. Pepper, Shirley Temple. Everyone laughed and drank and danced, and I felt amazing. I was with the cutest guy at the party, and he was with me. I really didn't think that life could get any better. But it did.

The party was at this really really big (like HUGE!) house in Bristol Oaks. Bristol Oaks is right next door to Hillsborough, where Biff is from. Biff said that his parents were out of town and did I want to see his house. Wow. Did I? I was a little scared because, you know, I'd never really "been" with a guy. Like I said, I'd kind of had a sheltered life. But Biff didn't seem like a guy. He was, like, this GREAT guy. Biff invited Clay and Bunny, too. We'd have a little after-party party, he said.

Biff's parents house was really, like, old. I don't mean it wasn't pretty, but it was kind of like a museum with all this old stuff that you were afraid to touch. His mother actually had ropes up in front of some of the rooms with little notes that said, "Biff, stay out." I guess she knew we were coming.

We went down to his basement. They had this great game room with pool and ping-pong tables, big couches, a big TV and stereo system, a bar—everything you could want.

We had a few drinks, and Clay and Bunny just kind of disappeared. Biff and I were sitting on the couch listening to a song. I think it was Coldplay. The one with the really cool video. I really liked the song. Then Biff kissed me. I didn't know what to think. I had been kissed before, you know, high school prom and all that. But not like this. It was like—WOW! These weird vibrations thundered through my body. Like I was melting or something. We just kissed and kissed and kissed. A lot of different songs kept playing—I remember wondering what Spotify list it was and what great taste he had in music.

By then we were lying on the couch. It was funny 'cuz Biff was still wearing that Budweiser suit. I started to giggle. Maybe it was the champagne. I dunno. All I could think was: Here I am in this incredibly beautiful house with this incredibly gorgeous guy, and he's wearing a Budweiser suit. I think I was a little scared, too. I wasn't sure if I should tell Biff that I had, you know, never "been" with a guy before. I decided I should. I didn't want him to think I was some sort of sex expert or anything. He was so sweet about it, too. He said he was surprised.

"But you are so sexy," he said.

I totally blushed. "No. I'm not."

"Yes, you are. Didn't you notice all the guys scamming on you in your little kilt tonight?"

"No."

"Yes. I can't believe you didn't know. Didn't you hear them telling me what a lucky dog I was to be with you?"

I couldn't believe my ears. Here I was feeling so lucky to be with him, and he's telling me how lucky he was to be with me.

"Biff, do you mind if we don't, you know, tonight? I mean, I really like you. Really, I do. But, we just met and I am kinda drunk. I'm just not sure I'm ready and . . ."

Biff cut me off.

"Cindy, I would love to make love to you tonight. But, if you want to wait, that's okey dokey with me."

I couldn't believe he was so understanding. God, he was just perfect.

"If you want," I continued, "we could, you know, sleep next to each other without, you know . . ."

"If that is what you want, babycakes, I think that would be rad."

Wow. We were pretty spent so we went upstairs to his room. He gave me a nightshirt to wear, and I fell asleep in his arms. Well, he fell asleep. I lay awake watching his face and looking around at his room—the room he grew up in. There were pictures of him as a kid. God, he was SO cute. I looked over at his face again. The lines were so perfect the way they moved together to form his incredible face. I was lying next to this incredible creature. And, for this night at least, he was my incredible creature.

The four of us spent the weekend at Biff's parent's house. They had a pool and a Jacuzzi and a tennis court. I never knew that places like that really existed. Sunday evening before heading back to school, Biff and I had sex. What can I say? It was SO great. He was so great. I felt so great. I was in love. I couldn't think straight. I didn't care about midterms or school or the sorority or life. If I would have died at that very moment, I would have died happy.

That was two years ago. Now I felt like wringing the little bastard's neck. I was standing outside the building where his sociology class was held.

21

It was humiliating, tracking down my boyfriend. The shithead. I just hoped nobody saw me.

"Cindy!"

Oh shit, it was Bunny.

"Hi, Bunny."

"Whatcha doing here? Waiting for Biff?"

I worked up an incredulous look on my face. "What? What are you talking about?"

"Isn't this where his sociology class is? Remember? We met him here a couple weeks ago."

"What? Here? Oh. Huh. Gee, maybe you are right. I'd forgotten all about that. Just passing by, you know."

"Sure. Going back to the house?"

"Um, a little later. Gotta meet with a professor."

"Okay. See ya."

"Yeah. Bye."

God, was that excruciating or what? Boy, was Biff gonna get it this time. I was really gonna give it to him. He just had to learn not to treat me this way. Never again. Nuh uh. He was gonna beg for mercy. Yes sirree bob.

There he was. Walking with . . . who was that? It looked like his sociology professor, Professor Hard Ass. Okay, so that wasn't her name. It was something… what? Professor DeVillier. Monique DeVillier. Everyone just called her Professor Hard Ass because, well, she was a total hard ass. For some reason, though, the guys just drooled over her. I could never figure it out. I mean, I guess she was good looking. And, okay, so she had a French name. Big whoop. What did she have that I didn't have? Biff Fuckface the fifth drooling all over her, that's what.

"Hey, baby." Finally, Biff spotted me. He stopped kissing Hardass's butt and sauntered on over to me.

"Hello." You can bet I was as cold as ice.

"Listen, sorry about Strada. Professor DeVillier could only give me two o'clock for office hours, and I just HAD to speak with her."

"Sure, Biff. I understand completely. No biggie. Really."

"That's my girl. Come on, let's grab a brewski."

Chapter Three
KATHY

War Council. Wars Council. War Council. It was all Maggie could talk about. Argh! I was sick of it. And what was it, really? I kept trying to figure that out.

"A business," Maggie said.

"A business?"

"Yeah. Like you go to them for help with your relationships."

"Like a therapist."

"No."

"Then what?"

"Well . . . like you go to a career counseling service for a job, right? Why not go to experts for relationship advice?"

"Like a therapist."

"No."

"Then what?"

"Like you hire a team of experts to be on your side."

"So, like the team from Mission: Impossible?"

"Yes, exactly, like if the Mission: Impossible team handled relationships. Think of The Bachelor, Dr. Phil, and Mission: Impossible all rolled into one."

"Paramilitary relationship counselors?"

"Exactly."

"You're kidding?"

"No."

"You're kidding."

"No. Don't you see? It's just so logical."

"It's nutso."

"No, it isn't. Why should we be alone in a relationship when we can have a team on our side?"

"What about love?"

"Love is dead."

"When did you get so cynical?"

"I'm not cynical. I'm realistic. We didn't all marry our college sweethearts, Kathy. It's a war out there, and in a war, we need some support. That's why it is so logical. It's so fucking logical, I can't believe I didn't think of it earlier."

"Maggie, what has happened to you?"

"I've wised up. That's what."

Wised up. Hah. Wised up. Trying to make love logical. Love? Who was she trying to kid? And where did this all come from?

Then I remembered: the bridal shower. It was that stupid bridal shower that pushed her over the edge. I never should have made her go. Maggie has never been good at those types of events, but I thought it was important that she be there.

The shower was for a mutual friend from the communications department, where Maggie was now teaching, so, politically, it was a good idea for her to attend. That and Laura had been a friend of ours for a long time, and I thought she could use our support. It really wasn't Laura's fault that the shower was so excruciatingly bad, either. It just happened that she was marrying into a family with no taste.

Laura's fiancé, Tobias, is a very nice man from a very wealthy family. A newly wealthy family, shall we say. Tobias has six sisters, and they were throwing the shower. It was mostly their friends and family and a few people from the department. I knew that Laura really appreciated our being there.

Of course, all of these great rationalizations and good intentions were lost on Maggie.

The shower was about as tacky as they come. It was held in this monstrosity of a house in a brand new luxury development called Bristol Oaks. Funny, too, because it is right next to Hillsborough, which is where those with, shall we say, more established wealth reside. So, while Hillsborough's houses reflected an old-money WASP mentality (lots of polo shirts and loafers), the houses in Bristol Oaks attempted to reflect the newly acquired wealth of its inhabitants. The mentality seemed to be that if you couldn't get into the closed enclave that is old money, you might as well flaunt the new.

Me, I like living in the city. Most of our friends live in the city. When you have lived in a city as long as we have, you tend to forget the suburban mentality. Not like we're snobs or anything. Well, maybe we are. I don't know. I just know that Brian and I will probably never leave the city. We love it. Every once in awhile, I think how nice it would be to have some real outdoor space, but then I go out to the suburbs and listen to the conversations and realize that the city is just fine.

The conversation at this party was especially inane. They salivated over the bizarre salmon mousse cake we had for lunch, cooed over the interminable party games (who invented those things, anyway?), then settled down to ooohand-aaah over the gifts.

Actually, the conversations were quite fascinating, not in a scintillating way, but in terms of figuring out who these women were and how they thought. I mean, let's face it, I became a psychologist because human nature fascinates me. I like to figure out just how people got to where they are. What processes lie behind their thoughts. These silly women were definitely grist for the mill.

As Laura continued opening her presents under the watchful eye of the six sisters, the women finally started talking about their lives. Okay, I thought, now this would be interesting. As I became more and more enthralled, Maggie, helped along by the champagne they'd so graciously served, really began to lose it.

The women all seemed to be dressed in Kardashian-inspired attire and had bizarrely plumped-up lips enhanced by lipstick that matched their nails. It was enough that I started to wonder if there was a bridal shower dress code somewhere and when it became fashionable to have lips that looked like they might flop around on their own if deprived of water.

Anyway, the fish-lip women went on and on about their husbands' careers, how much they earned, their new homes, their new decorators, their new rings, how many carats were in their new rings, and what schools their children were attending. They then proceeded to complain incessantly about their husbands, who seemed to spend all their time on the golf course.

Maggie listened intently to all of this and, unfortunately, decided to make a toast. I wasn't sure how many glasses of champagne she'd downed (the catering staff made sure they were never empty), but it must have been plenty. She looked a little unsteady and wavered a bit as she stood, but she made it. Then she cleared her throat. Laura looked up. The watchful sisters looked up. The fish-lips looked up. Maggie lifted her glass and said, "To love... to the death of love. Love is dead. I knew it all along."

There was a stunned silence as Maggie sat back down, looking very satisfied. The women, save Laura, looked shocked. Laura looked over at me and grinned. I smiled back. I knew then I had been right in thinking it was a good idea to attend the shower.

It took me awhile to figure out how Maggie had taken the events of that shower to come up with "love is dead." I mean, why did she take those silly women so seriously?

Then I remembered: Bill. When would she EVER get over him? It had been a year or so since he had left, and Maggie still didn't understand. She just didn't understand. Why, in her mind, had Bill not fought for their love? Why was the job in Tokyo more important than she was? We kept trying to tell her to move on, but she couldn't. Her latest theory (we'd been through more than a dozen) was obviously that love was dead.

Maggie saw the women at the shower as proof positive that she was right. She saw them as having used love to get their marriages, their houses, their decorators, etc. In a strange way, I think she admired them for using love so pragmatically. She had been willing to give up everything to just be with Bill while these women had used their love for material gain. Sick, I know, but you have to understand how Maggie thinks and also how the breakup with Bill devastated her.

Maggie is one of those people for whom logic is everything. If it is logical, she can deal with it. If it isn't logical, she will study it, analyze it and obsess upon it until it fits—until it is logical. She will make it logical. Force it. The best mental image I have is that of Maggie forcing a square peg into a round hole and saying "fit, damn it. Be logical."

Silly, isn't it? But this is the way she deals with life.

Personally, I think that if we made everything logical, life would be pretty darn dull. All that is magical and wonderful about the world is illogical. People are basically illogical beings. That's what is so wonderful about them. Machines are logical. People are not. If you want to deal with people and not machines, then you have to accept a little messiness.

Maggie hates messiness. You should see her apartment. Neat as a pin. A place for everything and everything in its place. My house will never be like that. I grew up in that. My mother's house was one of those museum-type places where you were not allowed to actually sit anywhere. I always swore I would have a house where people could be comfortable. When I was a kid, I hated that none of my friends wanted to come over and hang out at my house, which is probably why I love having people over to our place now. I love it. Brian and I have created a great house. A great big comfortable messy house.

Anyway, back to Maggie and the logic thing.

Bill leaving was not logical to Maggie. Bill telling her that he would be with other women after he left was not logical to Maggie. She saw

their love as this pure and wonderful phenom-
enon. In her mind, it was logical and perfect. They
were in love. They were together. It was simple.

And he fed into that. Bill was always telling
her how great she was—how beautiful, intelligent,
and special. How perfect they were together.
"Totally matched physically, emotionally, and
intellectually." Hard not to roll your eyes at that
one. But she bought it. They were perfect.

You want to know the truth? They weren't
perfect. Maggie has such a tendency to see
things in black and white that she sees her time
with Bill as being great and her life now as being
miserable. Neither is true. Maggie grew up the
years she was with Bill. Bill helped her grow into
herself—to see herself—but it isn't like it wouldn't
have happened without him. She was at a point
where she was a little scattered (okay, like off the
map), and he helped her to believe in herself.
And then he left.

Bill wrote every couple weeks but never gave
any clue that he had changed his mind. Maggie
held on. She lived for those emails and texts,
looked for any sign in them that he thought he
had made a mistake. She would analyze them,
looking for any suggestion of hidden feeling,
any indication that she hadn't been wrong—that
they had been special, that she was special.

It was so sad to watch. I couldn't believe that
Maggie—brilliant, volatile, independent Maggie—
had become so insecure. Anybody who has ever
known her knows that Maggie is a truly unique

and special person. Bill didn't make her those things. Why couldn't she see that?

The worst thing that Bill did, in my opinion, was tell her he would visit. It gave her hope. Hope that he would return. It cut her off from finding someone else. She had men falling all over her, but she either didn't give them the time of day or, if she did get involved, she at once decided they weren't Bill—and Bill was returning. She even kept his shaving cream and toothbrush sitting in her meticulously neat medicine cabinet. I know. I check every time I visit.

I am not saying that Bill is a bad person. I am not into bashing Bill. Enough of Maggie's friends bash him that I don't really need to. I always wondered about that. Why do people feel the need to bash the ex-whatever after a breakup? Again, I don't really believe there are any black-and-white issues when it comes to people. We're messy. We do stupid things. That's life.

I actually thought Bill was quite a likable fellow. Very intelligent, well read, a great conversationalist. But he wasn't a god, either. He wasn't this perfect fantasy creature Maggie made him out to be. I don't know what it is about him that made him want to leave, but he did. We all assumed Maggie would learn from it and move on. Stretch her wings.

But she didn't. Maggie closed up. Her pride took over. I think she was somehow embarrassed that she had offered to go with him, and he had turned her down. It just wasn't logical. To her, all the things she was feeling were not logical. It hurt too much. That was about where she was when we went to that fateful bridal shower.

After the shower, Maggie became a woman obsessed. She was still at UC Berkeley teaching business communications part-time as an adjunct professor and began grilling her colleagues on interpersonal communications and relationships. What theories were current. What books she should investigate. She then turned on my colleagues in the psychology department. She read every book on the subject. She started dating again. Unfortunately, her poor dates and short-lived relationships became test cases for her "experiments on love." My dinner parties became forums for debate on the issues she was exploring. She was essentially turning her pain into an academic research project.

I didn't realize how far she'd gone, however, until my last dinner party. I had purposefully asked Brian to bring along his friend Nick. I had met Nick on several occasions and thought he seemed like a good guy. A little unconventional, perhaps, but maybe that was what Maggie needed. I couldn't help it, couldn't help setting her up. I wanted her to be happy. I wanted to stop listening to the Bill theories. It can get on your nerves after a while. And I thought she and Nick might really hit it off.

I guess I was wrong—at least on her end—as she didn't give him even the slightest glance. I think he kind of liked her, though. He looked at her enough. And he got this quizzical look and little smile on his face as he watched every word that came out of her mouth.

The words that came out of her mouth were another thing. She started in again on this "War Council" stuff. "Love is dead" had somehow led to this idea of paramilitary relationship counselors. I started visualizing paratroopers swooping down on unsuspecting couples . . .

"Ma'am. How are you today?"
"Umm. Fine."
"Is this the guy?"
"Yeah."
"Sir. We hear you are having trouble committing."
"Who? Me?"
"Yes. You. The lady here has a problem with that. What are you going to do about it?"
"I don't know. I'm, well, I feel I'm too young to settle down and . . ."
"WRONG ANSWER!"
"I, uh . . ."
"Would you like a shot from the taser?"
"No!"
"Then we would like you to commit to this lady here."
"Um. Okay. Honey, do you want to, um, live together?"
"NOT GOOD ENOUGH. Try again."
"Um. Okay. Honey, do you want to, um, marry me?"

"Oh yes! Thank you, War Council paratroopers!"
"Congratulations. We'll be going now."

I tuned back in to find Maggie trying to sell the War Council as a business concept. A council of experts who take your side in the relation-ship battlefield, she was saying. All this ammu-nition stuff. "So logical," she kept saying. "People are starved for something like this. Think of the possibilities."

The idea was so incredibly cynical. What was she trying to prove? That she was never in love?

I looked around the dinner table to see what the response was. Everyone attacked the idea. I'm sure they thought she was joking. It had to be a joke, right? Another one of her little theories being tested. I hoped she was joking. I prayed she was joking. Unfortunately, I knew she wasn't.

I looked over at Brian. He was smiling. He loves it when she does this. I tell him he encour-ages her—like the children—but he just smiles. Sometimes I think he spends too much time with those rats.

At some point, Mike made a crude remark about casual sex and rugby being the only two things that made life bearable. Monique came at him with her fork, but Hallie managed to stop her before she broke any skin. Randy started hum-ming some song about love and romance from an old Audrey Hepburn movie. Nick picked it up. Some French love song that Edith Piaf sang. They swigged at the wine bottle and grabbed at the baguette. It was pretty silly, but at least they got everybody to laugh. Everyone but Maggie.

Maggie was annoyed. I could tell. She tried to get them back to talking about this "War Council" stuff, but they were already debating the artistic merits of French music during the occupation. I was glad.

Then Maggie got this funny look on her face. She started looking around at the people at the table. What was she thinking now? With her mind, it could be anything. I was just hoping she would get over this latest episode quickly. I never wanted to hear about the War Council again.

Chapter Four
MAGGIE

Pow. I was ready. Phase Two of the War Council. I had the idea. I had the strategies. Now I just needed my personnel. Every general needs troops, right? I knew who I wanted. It was just a matter of how to persuade them just how logical it really was.

I started with Kathy. I read her some ads I had written for the War Council. I knew they were great. She had to see the logic.

"We'll do what books and analysis can't—tackle the problem from all sides—rationally." I put down my iPad. "So, which do you like better?"

"Maggie, please don't do this."

"What?"

"I don't want to talk about it."

"Talk about what?"

"This War Council stuff. When are you going to drop it?"

"Why should I drop it? It's a great idea."

"Never mind."

"What?"

"How's your latte?"

"Don't try to change the subject."

"I don't like the subject. I am sick of the subject. I never want to hear about the War Council again."

"Why not?"

"Because it's ridiculous. It's cynical, unrealistic, and I just wish you would get over him without taking it out on the world."

"Get over who?"

"Who do you think? Bill."

"This has nothing to do with Bill." (Can you believe she thought this had to do with Bill?)

"Bullshit."

"Kathy!"

"Well, that's what it is. This is all about some vendetta you have against Bill."

"This has nothing to do with Bill. I'm over him. And don't give me that look."

"What about your other theories?"

"This is different. This is a logical response to a need. Don't you see how needed a service like this is? People are crying out for help. We will help them. And we can make some good money doing it."

Kathy and I were sitting at Café Strada. We met there once a week. It was the perfect place for my War Council research. I could see all the couples coupling or not coupling, and I knew they needed me. They needed the War Council.

Kathy was proving harder to convince than I planned. I have to admit it pissed me off. Can you believe that she thought the War Council was because of Bill? Please. It was just so logical. She had to see that. The pure logic of it all.

I pulled up the list of books I had found on Amazon.

"Here, look at these. They show the need. And let me tell you, it's just a fraction of what's out there. *He's Just Not That into You. How to Spot a Commitment-phobe. Looking for Love in All the Wrong Places. Love Must Be Tough. Barriers to Intimacy. Games People Play. Chasing Loves: 10 Steps to a Happier Relationship. Light His Fire: How to Keep Your Man Passionately and Hopelessly in Love with You. Love and Power in a World Without Limits. The Cinderella Complex. Intimate Connections: The Clinically Proven Program for Making Close Friends and Finding a Loving Partner.* Oh, and this is the best—*How to Make a Man Fall in Love with You: The Failproof, Foolproof Method.* Look what it says on the back. 'Find the love of your life. Make the chemistry of love happen—at will. Meet your love's unconscious needs. Establish instant trust and rapport. Get him to say yes—so subtly he won't even know you've done it.'"

"Maggie. Those are garbage."

"Exactly. Because they just treat one person. The person in pain. We also go after the source. The person CAUSING the pain. We become involved."

"Maggie Maggie Maggie."

Kathy was getting that patronizing look that I hated so much. God, I hated that look. The look that said, "Oh, silly silly Maggie. I'm so perfect, and she's so silly." I hated that look. I must admit, though, that it really fueled me to prove her wrong—to prove to her that the War Council could work. That it was needed and could be successful.

"Kathy. I know you're a psychologist. And I know that you think you know it all, but just go along with me for a moment."

She sighed. "Fine."

Oooh. Now, she was getting that "Fine, I'll listen to you, but I still won't think it's a good idea" look. That REALLY steamed me. But this time I didn't let it get to me.

"Okay, then tell me: Why do you think those books are so popular?"

She got her know-it-all psychologist look. Like, "look at me, the professional."

"Because people are looking for answers from the outside instead of looking at themselves. It's easier to find excuses and to have rules dictated to you than to examine yourself. The people who buy these books are unhappy with themselves. Until they realize this and look for the reasons behind their unhappiness, they will follow the same patterns and not find the love or happiness they are seeking."

"Absolutely perfect," I said.

"What?"

"Perfect. I love it. Don't you see how much you could help people with that advice? Think of all the poor people going to these awful books for advice that you could help with what you just told me. You could help people learn to like and love themselves. The way you do in therapy. Except now you would be part of a larger unit. Think of it as flipping group therapy around. Instead of one therapist and many patients—it's one patient and many experts."

Kathy sat there for a moment. I'd made her think. Yes! I knew I'd gotten to her. Ha! Logic. And Ego. Works every time. If you appeal to a person's ego through logic, you'll always come out on top. Try it sometime.

"Why are you doing this to me, Maggie?"

"I want you to be a part of the War Council."

"Why me?"

"Because you are perfect for it. Don't you see? You're a really good psychologist and would be a valued member of the team."

She was wavering.

"But..."

"Look, Kathy, I think this will work. I think people need the service we could provide. When you see a need, you fill it. I see a need."

I looked around for something that would help me to make my point. I saw a girl sitting all by herself at Café Strada. Now that was a rare occurrence. Nobody sits alone at Café Strada. Other cafés, yes. Not Strada. It was one of those stupid unwritten norms that everybody followed. She had been stood up. I knew it.

"Now look at that poor girl." I pointed to the girl sitting alone.

"So?"

"She's alone."

"So?"

"So, let's think of her as our typical War Council client."

"Uh huh."

"She's been stood up. Poor girl. She's pretty but lacking in confidence. I'm thinking she has a boy-friend, but now he's acting kind of shitty. Maybe telling her he needs some space. Standing her up occasionally. Let's say she's graduating soon. Thinking about the future. Wants to get married maybe. He's thinking about spreading his wings. She's unhappy. She could hire the War Council."

"What about him?"

"Who cares?"

"Who cares?"

"We're only hired by one partner. Like I said, it's a war. You don't fight on both sides of a war."

"What if—I'm being hypothetical here—what if she's a neurotic mess who's obsessively jealous of her boyfriend, and he's a great guy?"

"So? He didn't hire us."

"This is so cynical."

"Think of us as lawyers."

"More like mercenaries."

"Okay. But I really don't think a neurotic obsessive would be rational enough to realize she requires help with her relationship. We'll get the victims. The people who know they're on the wrong end of the relationship power struggle."

"Why does it have to be a power struggle?"

"Kathy, every relationship isn't perfect, equal, 50-50, whatever. Most aren't. We aim to help the people who are weakened by the hold their partner has over them."

"You are nuts."

"Are you in?"

"I must be nuts."

"Think of it as an experiment. If it goes wrong, you can write a book on it and make millions."

"I'm hoping you are wrong."

"Great. Prove me wrong. All I ask is that you try to make it work."

"I suppose I could do that. Who else is going to be part of this?"

"I am thinking Monique, Mike, Hallie, and Randy."

"And how do you intend to get them to agree to this?"

"Logic. Works every time."

I found Monique coming out of her office. Monique tended to be easy to find. Office. Library. Home. If she wasn't at one of those three places, she was probably en route. As usual, there were approximately ten male students following her. Incredible. Almost 40 and the toughest teacher on campus, and all the 20-something alpha male students idolized her. When she saw me, she shooed the students away, and we found a nearby bench where I began my pitch.

I had decided to zero in on Monique's academic background to gain her support. I read her more of the book titles I had gathered in my search: *How to Make a Man Fall in Love with You. Men Who Can't Love. Women Men Love, Women Men Leave. Secrets About Men Every Woman Should Know. The Good Girl Syndrome. The Secrets Men Keep. Why Men Are the Way They Are. Men Who Hate Women and the Women Who Love Them. What Men Don't Tell Women...* I knew they'd get her venom up. And they did.

"Propagandistic products perpetuating the patriarchal paradigm."

Okay, so Monique was prone to alliteration.

"Sickening, aren't they? That's what the War Council is out to destroy. Instead of turning to this sludge, they can turn to us—to you—to guide them in their endeavors and help them to assert their womanhood in the best possible way."

She pondered.

"This War Council abstraction might provide some intriguing material for my next paper. It concerns the subversive means by which a capitalist society continues to demean women's worth. I had been pondering the subject in terms of the workplace, but this love paradigm might prove piquant."

"So, are you in?"

"Why not? The students this semester are proving to be rather doltish. I could use some stimulation."

♡ ♥ ♡

Hallie and Randy were next. I arranged to meet them one night at a local pub. Good food and microbrews. I figured I would pit the two of them against each other. You know, divide and conquer. Not only were they great minds on their own, but they held the two most disparate viewpoints I had ever known. Hallie was the cynical strategist while Randy was a romantic idealist. I thought that if I could get them to argue against each other, they'd beg to sign up. Logic. Ego. Right?

Wrong. Hallie began defending Randy's point of view while Randy began defending Hallie's. It was kind of cute, actually. I looked deeper for an explanation as there definitely was ego involved but not what I had bargained for. Then it occurred to me—it was the collective ego speaking. The bond that marriage creates. They'd been married for ten years, but no one had ever expected it to last. They were too different. Too disparate in their thinking. But the marriage had lasted, and they were pretty damn proud of that fact. That was the ego I was getting now, so I changed my attack.

"Hallie. Randy." I looked at each of them earnestly. "Not only are you both experts in your fields—sterling examples of critical thinking—but you serve as a model for working relationships."

They smiled at each other, and I knew I had them.

♡ ♥ ♡

Mike was my last conquest. Now that I had Kathy, Monique, Hallie, and Randy, I was feeling pretty confident. And let's face it: Mike was a dude. Not that Randy wasn't, but again, I was dealing with a collective unit in that case. Here I was dealing with raw male ego.

I found Mike down by the rugby field where a lot of squatty guys in striped shirts and little shorts pummeled each other while running up and down the field. How appropriate. Mike was yelling at one of them.

"GET THE FUCK OUT OF THAT CORNER! BUD, GO FOR THE BALL. GO FOR THE BALL!"

"Hey, Mike."

He gave me a quizzical look. "Maggie. What the hell are you doing here?"

"I just wanted a minute of your time."

"Minute's all you got. Go."

"Well, I wanted to talk to you about that War Council idea from Kathy's dinner party last Friday."

"War Council? Don't remember it. Refresh my memory. Just a second . . . BASH THE BASTARD, CONRAD! WHAT ARE YOU WAITING FOR?" Back to me. "Sorry. Go ahead."

"The idea about the paramilitary relationship counselors?"

"Relationship counselors?" Mike made what I would describe as a goose-egg sound. "Men don't worry about this shit. We go for what we want and, well…" Then he winked.

I smiled. "Funny. Monique said you'd say that. Said you wouldn't want to do it because you were afraid."

"Hard Ass said that? Hah! LATERAL! LATERAL, YOU WUSS. I'm not afraid of anything, least of all what Miss—excuse me, *Professor* DeVillier might think."

"That's what I thought. Except… well, I was thinking that you might not want people—poor unsuspecting young people—indoctrinated. All those men turned 'sensitive'…"

"So what?"

"Wouldn't you love the chance to do a little indoctrinating of your own? The chance to show people the inner workings of the real man?"

"Yeah. I'm just not all that into that communicating shit."

"That's not what it's about, Mike. You would be actively involved. Not just talking, but like I said, we're going to use military principles to fight the war in the field where it should be fought, not in the therapist's office. Mike, I gotta tell you—your services as a captain in our little army would be vital."

"Captain, eh?"

Logic. Ego. Bingo.

"Yessir. You could train men and women your way. The way you train these fine young men out here."

Just as I was saying that, one of the squatty bodies out on the field squished into another squatty body and blood came squirting out of his nose. Ewww.

"PHIL! PHIL, GET A TOWEL TO SIMMONS. LEARN TO TAKE A HIT BETTER, SIMMONS!"

The squatty body nodded and went right back into the game.

"Wow, Mike, I've gotta say that the way you mold these young men is simply fabulous. Wouldn't it be great if you could help some of those not gifted in rugby?"

Mike screwed up his face real tight. I think that meant he was thinking.

"Ah, what the fuck. These assholes haven't scored all season. Someone might as well. Get it?"

Mike slapped me hard on the back. I got it. I got it, and I have to admit the slap on the back killed. But I had him, and now the War Council was complete.

♡ ♥ ♡

I was walking on air the next week when I met Kathy at Café Strada.

"Well, I got 'em."

She looked morose. "Everyone?"

"Every last one."

"Damn," she said. "And don't give me that look, Maggie. You know I don't want this to work."

"I am going to prove to you just how great this idea is."

"I'll see it when I believe it. And how are you going to find the time to teach your classes?"

"Please, I'm still an adjunct, remember? All I'm teaching is the graduate seminar this semester."

Kathy started to say something but then glanced behind me and got a surprised look on her face. I knew that look. It wasn't the look of real surprise. It was that fake set-up kind of happy surprise. And then I saw him. What's-his-name from her dinner party. Oh, Kathy, what was this? Didn't she see I wasn't going to have time for dating? I mean, please, now that the War Council was ready to roll, it would be taking all of my time. Would she never give up?

"Maggie, you remember Nick."

Nick.

"Yeah, yeah. Hi, Nick."

Nick, right. And, okay, so he was kind of nice looking. He definitely had a nice smile. One of those smiles that kind of twinkles. I hate twinkling smiles. Except that his was okay. Not as stupid as most twinkling smiles. He also had blue eyes and unruly dark brown hair. It was a nice combination. Somewhat pedestrian, I suppose, but on him it worked. He was certainly no Bill. And, like I said, I was going to be way too busy with the War Council to ever get to know him.

Chapter Five
NICK

Sweet mystery of love I have found her. There she sat. A vision. And such passion—it was like there was fire flying out of her eyes. Her dark hair waved as she shook her head vigorously. She wore a blue sweater. She'd had on a red sweater at the dinner party. I think I liked the blue better—it brought out the specks of gold in her green eyes—and it was a little more snug. Yes, I think the blue was definitely superior.

Would I tell her? How would I tell her? Why would I tell her? And why were these thoughts spinning around in my brain? Oh, the dilemma that faced me. I didn't remember feeling like this in years, if ever. Giddy. And nervous. Sweaty palms, the whole bit. Shit, this was ridiculous. Just walk up to them. Geez, you're 37 years old. You're beyond all of this, right?

Just then Kathy looked up. She looked at me and nodded like, "Come on, you schmuck." We had arranged the meeting. Well, I had requested it, and she told me she thought it was a good idea. I just had to see Maggie again. What was unusual was I didn't quite know why or how. I mean, I know how to approach a woman, but not this woman. There was something about her—something unattainable, mysterious, unyielding, fascinating… Something that said—yes, I may be the one, but no, you may not have me. Something that made me say: Why not? Which, of course, triggered something that said: Don't blow it. Which, naturally, triggered something that said: SHUT UP! Why are you obsessing? You never obsess about women.

So why was I obsessed? I didn't think it was the unattainable part. I've never been into conquests. I am into women. I love women, the way they're built, both mentally and physically. I love getting to know women and discovering what is unique about each one. And Maggie fascinated me like no woman had in a very long time.

I actually think it was this War Council stuff that really hooked me. I mean, that was really funny—a paramilitary group that counsels troubled relationships? That's great stuff. What kind of mind would come up with that? A fascinating mind, that's what. A mind that thinks about life and love.

And the passion with which she pretended to believe in it all. It was brilliant. This was a mind that I wanted to get to know better. And, luckily, the package that went with that mind was pretty darn terrific.

51

I started toward the table. Kathy actually looked grateful for my arrival. It made me wonder what they had been talking about. Maggie looked, well, not particularly pleased that I had interrupted them. I really wondered what they had been talking about.

"Hi. Maggie, you remember Nick."

"Yeah, yeah. Nick. Hi."

Ah, that voice. Those words. God, she was just beautiful.

"Have a seat. I'm going to run to the bathroom so you two chat for a while," Kathy said, before bolting for the bathroom. Maggie shot her a look that could kill but then turned back to me, and the look wasn't quite so lethal. I just wish it hadn't been so patronizing.

"So, you're a friend of Brian's."

"Yep. Known him for years."

"You a rat?" She laughed. I didn't know what the heck she was talking about.

"A rat?"

"Yeah. I thought the only things Brian saw outside of Kathy and the kids were rats."

"Oh, well, then no, I'm not a rat." I could see she was going to be tougher than I thought. "Brian and I play tennis together."

"Tennis?" The tone said "tennis, how bourgeois." I was definitely the toad in this scenario.

"Yeah, you play?"

"Nope."

"Oh." Now that was scintillating. Come on, man, come up with something brilliant. "Too bad."

"You at Berkeley?"

"Yes, I am." Aha. A link. Something in common.

"What are you teaching?"

"I'm not teaching. I'm a student."

"A student?" Another disdainful look—this one to size up my age.

"Yep, a student," I said.

"In what?"

"French literature."

"Ah, the Edith Piaf songs."

"Yep."

Okay, so we had not developed a sparkling repartee. For some reason, my usual ready wit had buried itself in my book bag.

"PhD?"

"Nope. Another bachelor's."

Again, the calculating of the age was obvious in her eyes.

"Why?"

"I'm not into the academic bullshit that comes with graduate work."

She arched an eyebrow. It was something.

"Something of an impractical major," she said. For someone my age, she meant. Don't worry. I wasn't insulted.

"They've all been." That'll throw her.

"All?" It did. Both eyebrows arched.

Aha. A spark of interest. Kathy arrived. Damn. I could sense that Maggie was finally becoming intrigued.

Maggie looked almost guilty for starting to enjoy herself but, making excuses, scurried off.

What the hell were they talking about before I got there? I asked Kathy.

"That stupid War Council," she said.

"The story she told at the dinner party?"

"No, that's the problem. It's not a story. She really believes in it and wants to make it work."

I laughed. "Paramilitary relationship counselors?"

"Yep. We'll be the Mission: Impossible team of love."

"Who's gonna be Tom Cruise?" Kathy shot me a look. "I'm sorry. So how, exactly, will it work?"

"Who knows? It's an awful idea and illustrates everything that is wrong with a world where relationships are based on 'The Bachelor.' Can you believe she wants us to become involved in people's relationships? Make them logical. Even worse, she wants us to only take one side and refuses to see that there are two sides to every relationship. I mean, come on! There is no right and wrong in love."

"Depends on her definition of wrong."

"Don't start. I know you think this is a big joke, and it is—really. I just have to figure out how to make Maggie believe that." Kathy sighed. "If she could just get over Bill."

Bill? Uh oh. Danger signs. Flashing warning bells. I was cool.

"Who's Bill?"

Kathy looked over as if surprised she was speaking to me. As if suddenly realizing she was spilling her guts to a complete stranger.

To be honest, we didn't know each other very well. We had known of each other since Brian and I started playing on a USTA tennis team a few years earlier, but I had only gotten to know Kathy recently. Still, I was intrigued and wanted her to continue.

"I'm sorry," Kathy said. "This must be so boring."

"No, really, it isn't. Go ahead." I looked as earnest and well meaning as I could. Well, I was.

Kathy considered me for a minute and decided to continue. It seemed like she needed to get it off her chest. She filled me in on the story of Maggie and this Bill fellow and how it had led to the War Council idea. I didn't think Bill sounded like such a bad guy. Not a guy to mourn for two years but not a bad sort in general. It sounded like he knew what he wanted and went for it. I thought he was an idiot for giving up someone like Maggie but, then again, everybody thought I was an idiot for leaving Tina.

It was ten years ago. I was 27, and up until that point in my life, I had done everything that was expected of me. I was the good kid, the kind of kid who didn't rebel in high school. I was too busy working. My family was one of those middle-class suburbia types. My dad was a dentist, and mom was a housewife. We had a nice life but were by no means wealthy. And, from as long as I can remember, I worked. Summers,

Christmas vacations, after school. My dad said it was good training for real life—Puritan work ethic and all that.

When I wasn't working odd jobs, I was working on my studies—gotta get good grades to get into the good schools—or playing on the tennis team (which looked good on college applications). Of course, when it came to going to college, I went to the local school: UC Irvine. I mean, why spend money on things such as dorms and food when there was a perfectly good university 15 minutes from home?

I majored in computer science. Good practical major. The computer business was booming, so why not jump on the bandwagon (my Dad's thoughts)? It wasn't even that bad. I enjoyed working with computers. They didn't talk back or tell me what to do. And it's not that I want to paint this picture of a deprived youth. To tell the truth, I didn't really have any ideas of my own, so I just went along with what my folks wanted.

I met Tina my senior year of college. She was gorgeous. She was in the theater department, and I thought she was so exotic—mostly because she was doing something SO impractical. I mean, what does one DO with a theater major? Tina had started out in acting but was turned off by all the artsy-fartsies (her word) constantly trying to outdo each other. She didn't have that kind of personality. Tina was more, well, like me. Middle class suburbanite. You know the type—she's the homecoming queen and everybody tells her she's gorgeous, so she decides to act. It wasn't really in her blood, though. By her senior year, she had gotten into doing the costumes. That was something she could relate to as she loved clothes. The funny thing is that she couldn't draw, so she would use these paper dolls to do the costume renderings. She was clever and she was beautiful.

I met Tina in the computer lab. That was my part-time job on campus, and Tina had decided she needed to learn more programs on the computer. She was that type. "It seems to me that it will be beneficial to learn how to use these machines." She was so theatrical. And yet practical. Practically theatric. Everything was an event.

And yeah, okay, it was her looks that first attracted me. Tina was incredibly petite but well built if you know what I mean. She would wear these very tight low-cut tops and what I learned later was a very advanced-for-its-time push-up bra. I would catch a glimpse of her cleavage as I leaned over to show her something on the keyboard and would get woozy every time. I mean, come on! I was the guy who was always either working or in the computer lab—boobs were a big big deal.

After a couple sessions in the lab, we began to talk about ourselves. I told her about all my plans—about how I was going to start my own computer business and make a ton of money. My dad and I had already talked about starting a business to provide computer software for dentists' offices. There'd been some crappy programs, but the dental field was a niche that really hadn't been well served, and we had high hopes for its success.

So anyway, I told Tina my plans, and she seemed to get more and more interested in me. Like I said, she was pretty practical for a theater major. So, with my lust for her body and her lust for my perceived future success, we became a couple.

By the time I was 27, we had been dating for more than five years. We (well, she) began talking marriage. It seemed to be the thing to do. I got the ultimatum and, since I had done everything else that was expected of me, it felt pretty natural to become engaged. So, we did. It was expected. My family loved Tina. We would get married and move into the development where my parents lived. By then, the business was really beginning to take off, so my life would be set. Or so I thought.

The summer of my 27th year, two major events changed my life. My father died. He was 55. It was one of those stories you always hear about. He was playing squash with his partner when he had a brain aneurysm and just fell dead on the court—55 fucking years old. He had been working since he was 15. His whole life.

My dad had recently told me that he was going to retire. That he could sell half the dental practice to a young associate and live off what we were making from the software company. He would finally get to enjoy life. He was building a boat—puttered in his garage every weekend on the damn thing. He wanted to sail around the world. My dad read *The Sea Wolf* when he was a kid and always had this dream of sailing around the world like Jack London. He was finally going to get to live his dream when he dropped dead on a squash court in Irvine, California.

The second event was the success of my company. It was already turning a profit, and we were getting numerous requests from dentists around the country for our software product. We were growing. Two months after my father's death, the offer came. A big software conglomerate wanted to buy my company. They offered me $20 million. $20 million. It wasn't humongous bucks by any means, but it was a nice sum of money. If I gave half to my mother, invested the rest of it carefully and didn't spend like an idiot, I could live off it for the rest of my life.

My life. Suddenly I wasn't sure what I wanted to do with my life. The man I had tried so desperately hard to please had just died. The money I wanted so desperately to earn had suddenly been offered to me on a silver platter. What were my options? Marry Tina? Buy a big house and live in the suburbs in a lifestyle that would force me to work the rest of my life so I could die at 55? Or maybe, just maybe, I could really live. I had never been out of the United States. I had never been free. Something just clicked inside me. I didn't want a lifetime of work. I didn't want the suburbs. And I didn't want Tina.

To say she was upset would be an understatement. This was a woman who had been a theater major, you will recall. Her temper tantrum will go down in the history books. Or the Academy Awards. Whatever, it was a doozy. Then, when that didn't work, she groveled. She begged me to stay and marry her. The more she pushed, the more I couldn't wait to get away. It was so sad, and I felt so guilty. It wasn't that I didn't want to be with her, it was that I didn't want to be with anybody. I wanted to float. I wanted to go and do things. To travel. To learn things that weren't practical. To meet new people and talk about things other than flash drives and dental charts. I wanted exotic.

I wished there had been room in my plans for Tina, but there just wasn't. I needed to do this on my own. To explore. I told her I wasn't sure if I would be back or not. I wanted to be honest with her. I didn't want the guilt of her waiting for me. I also didn't want her to think that I would be faithful—because one of the things I wanted to explore was the world of women.

♡ ♥ ♡

Three continents, four colleges, and five girlfriends later, I was at Berkeley majoring in French Literature. Still a rather logical (if not practical) fellow, I had decided to combine the learning of impractical subjects with my desire to travel. I knew myself. After a lifetime of structure, totally unstructured travel would be a jolt to my system. I also felt like I'd missed out on what college really offered–the chance to acquire knowledge you will never use in "real life." So, I studied Anthropology at the University of Wisconsin, which took me to Egypt; Music History at Indiana, which took me to Austria; Latin American Studies at UCLA, which took me to Uruguay and Brazil; and Art History at NYU, which took me to the wilds of New York City.

Each of these experiences brought with them an exciting, fascinating woman. New York brought two–I don't know what it is about New York City, but the relationships seem to have a shorter life span. I'm definitely a sequential monogamist, so they were all steady girlfriends for their time. And, when my program ended at each college, the leaving got easier–and harder. Although I cared for each of these women, I didn't really want to share the rest of my life with any one of them. That made it easier to do the actual breakup thing. What was harder was the feeling I got after leaving. It was a sad sort of melancholy that came out of the fact that I didn't want to share the rest of my life with any of these women. Why not? Like I said, they were all fascinating, exciting women, and I wasn't getting any younger.

Was it me? Was it timing? Was it them? I remember one of my girlfriends–one of the New

York girlfriends—putting a book on my doorstep about something called commitment-phobia. I had never heard of such a thing. It troubled me. For about two weeks. The feeling then passed as I began tackling the challenges that a new school brought.

And then there was Maggie. All my explorations of women had not prepared me for how I was feeling about this woman that I barely knew. I had to figure out a way to get to know her better. And then it hit me: The War Council.

"What?"

I realized I'd said it out loud. I must admit that, in my reverie, I had forgotten that Kathy was still there—pouting into her latte.

"The War Council," I repeated.

"What about it?"

"It's perfect."

She groaned. I continued, "No, listen. You want to prove the War Council wrong, right?"

"Right."

"To prove that there are two sides to every relationship."

"Right."

"And that love isn't logical."

"So…?"

"So, how about if we turn the War Council around on Maggie—without letting her know, of course."

A sly smile crept onto Kathy's face. "What are you saying?"

"I'm saying that I would like to hire the War Council to get to know Maggie better."

For the first time that day, I saw Kathy really smile. It was one a big, broad "damn, it's good to be alive" kind of smile. I returned the smile. She nodded. I nodded.

And thus, the anti-War Council War Council conspiracy was born over two double lattes at the Café Strada.

Chapter Six
MAGGIE

I had a mutiny on my hands. Okay, maybe not a real mutiny but definitely some dissension in the ranks. They were all still eager to be a part of the War Council idea. They just couldn't agree on what the War Council's goals or tactics should include. Hey, it was my War Council. I knew what the goals and tactics were. What was wrong with these people?

I had assembled them all in our new office. It wasn't really an office as much as one of the rooms reserved for faculty experiments at the university. Right now, we just had four empty walls and some chairs. But there was potential. I had requisitioned the office space for the War Council when I first came up with the idea. I wrote in the required prospectus that I was doing an experiment on group dynamics in the business environment. Okay, so I lied. Not really, though. I mean, we were running the War Council as an experiment, right? And it was potentially lucrative so that filled the business part. Plus, we were a group, am I right?

In any case, I had my office. I had my troops. I had my troops in my office. And they were arguing. This was not going as expected. After (I will admit) some initial defensiveness, I decided to sit back and see what they had to say. I was going to try not to control where they wanted to take my baby. I mean, I did pick them for their disparate views, right? They could only add to what I had already formulated. So, I sat back and listened.

Mike was the first to speak. "I think this idea of coercing people into marriage is a bit limited."

Kathy agreed. "Yes. We could help people get to know each other. For instance, if someone has, say, seen or met someone briefly that they are interested in, the War Council could help them initiate the relationship."

Mike nodded. "Or get them laid."

Monique snorted. "Oh, please."

"What?"

"Perpetuating the stereotype a bit, aren't we?"

"Hey, I am just giving you my perspective. That's why I'm here, right? Well, women want commitment. I'm just saying that men don't want that. We just want to get laid."

"That is the biggest load of sexist drivel I have heard."

"What?"

"That women's sole desire is for marriage while men's is for sex."

"Well…" said Mike.

"Nonsense," said Monique.

"Okay, then what do you think?"

"I think there are women who just want a piece of ass…"

Everybody's eyebrows shot up. The gathering was definitely perking up.

"…and I think there are men who want to coerce women into marriage."

"Why would a man want marriage when he can get it for free?"

"Oh, please. Men obtain much more from marriage than women do," said Monique.

"Like what?"

"Like free labor. Women work equivalent daily schedules outside the home and yet continue to perform most of the household chores."

"As well they should," said Mike with a smile.

Before chairs started to fly, I decided to stick my two cents in. "Listen, when I came up with the idea, I decided that it would not be gender specific. A man might want to help his partner commit as much as any woman."

Kathy piped in. "Well, then what about helping people—of both sexes—get, for lack of a better word, laid? I don't think it's wrong to open it up a bit."

"Well, sure," I said, going with the flow. "Any other suggestions?"

"I'm kind of curious as to how people will pay for these services," said Hallie, always practical. "I mean, would helping someone get laid cost the same as helping someone coerce their partner into commitment?"

"What about trying to do some real good here?" suggested Randy, who had been silent up until this point. "I mean, what about helping a troubled marriage? Or helping people to understand the underlying problems within their relationship? We might actually save some couples from the trauma of breaking up—especially when there are children involved."

Sweet Randy. Sweet, idealistic, misinformed Randy. What a sap. He only knew from old movies where everyone was happily ever after at the end.

Everyone took a moment to give him a look and then started in with their own ideas. We finally decided that everyone could be accommodated, and that Hallie would make up a price chart for the different services we would provide. We did draw the line at helping people cheat, even though there are even apps for that these days. Too cynical—even for me.

Until we had our first client, that was the best we could do. We adjourned and the next day I placed an ad on the campus website:

Love life on the skids?
Trouble meeting the One?
Problems getting your partner
to live up to your expectations?
You want marriage and your partner
wants "space"?

Hire the War Council. In the battle of the sexes, we're all the artillery you need.

I only had to adapt the ad a bit from my original concept. The naysayers—well, Kathy—suggested that no one would answer the ad. We had agreed that if that happened (but I knew it wouldn't), we would do a freebie for publicity. Hallie pointed out that the best marketing would probably come from word of mouth, and we might need to achieve some success with the Council's tactics before we could count on a continual flow of customers. Whatever. I mean, please, who wouldn't want to hire the War Council? It was such a great idea. There was such great need. It was just so damn logical.

I was on such a high after placing the ad in the *Daily Cal's* advertising office that I didn't even notice that Nick guy was standing just outside in the quad. I practically ran right into him. What a coincidence, huh? Well, not such a coincidence, I suppose, as the quad is where everyone congregates between classes, and he was a student, after all.

He smiled that twinkling smile. I suppose he wasn't *so* bad.

"Well, hi, Maggie," he said. "I think this is the first time I have seen you on campus."

"I guess that's right." I did kind of wonder why Nick always seemed like such a knucklehead around me. I mean, here was a guy with five degrees, and he could barely finish a sentence.

"So, uh, where are you headed?" he asked.

"Back to my office in Sproul Hall."

"How about that? I'm headed in the same direction. Mind if I join you?"

"Not at all."

"Great."

"Yeah, great." Like I said, total knucklehead. And he had that "gosh, gee, golly" kind of look. Uh oh. I knew that look. It's the same look I used to get when I was first getting to know Bill.

Like I mentioned, I fell in love late in life. I was 24—almost 25—and going through an identity crisis. Up until that point, everything in my life had been academically oriented. School had always come really easy for me. I mean, it was just so damn logical. Logic and ego. Let's face it, professors are basically egotistical creatures, so if you appealed to their ego through logic... need I say more?

I whizzed through undergrad in three years. Piece of cake. By my sophomore year, I had even developed a system for taking exams that was working quite well. I later sold it to the Cal basketball team (before their most successful season, I might add).

I then finished my master's in one year. That was an even bigger piece of cake. I had completed the coursework for my doctorate when I burned out. I was almost 25 and hadn't done anything but deal with this little world my whole life. I began to feel so limited. The "ivory tower," a colleague of mine used to call it. It was, and I felt trapped inside it. I wasn't sure I wanted to continue living in that tower and finish my doctorate or what it was I did want to do with my life.

My doctoral advisor said I should take a year off. Get my academic spirit back. They use corny phrases like that—academic spirit? Please.

I decided to take a job that was completely mindless, so I worked in a local café-bookstore. For some reason, I couldn't bring myself to actually leave Berkeley. It had been home for too many years, and besides, this was just a break, right? So, I stayed. But I did stay away from campus and worked and, well, mostly I just kind of loafed.

Naturally, I was bored within a month. Was that all there was to life? Soul-sucking jobs or academia? What a choice. The problem was that nothing in the "real world" interested me. My field was organizational communications, and I had spent a lot of time studying how businesses functioned and the group dynamics of business communications, so theoretically I could work in the corporate world, but all that research had just shown me that the business world was ten times more tedious than academia. So, I was stuck.

Not that the café-bookstore was that bad. Some interesting types used to come in. It's funny how regulars develop in a place like that. And, yes, it was not lost on me that it was my year off, and I was analyzing the clientele of a small business. Old habits, am I right? I actually ended up doing a lot of research for my dissertation there. Mostly, though, I just people watched.

And then, one day, HE came in. And then he became a regular. Yes, Bill. Wow. Even now when I think about him and that first moment, I get a chill that runs throughout my body. I had just about given up on men when he can into my life. At that time, it seemed the choice was between frat boys with over-active hormones or stuffy intellectuals spouting Roland Barthes. Bill was neither. He was just... Bill.

I noticed him the first time he came in. He would come in every day around 9 a.m. to read the *New York Times*—yes, he still read the news-PAPER—and drink an espresso. Like, he didn't even drink fluffy cappuccinos or caffe lattes—no, he had the real thing. Espresso. And he would wear these old gray t-shirts like he'd just been running or whatever it was he did in the mornings. He'd come in, buy the *New York Times* from me, then meander into the café for the espresso.

It was his face that I noticed first. He had this beautiful black hair and brown eyes with long black lashes that completely encircled his eyes. It was a beautiful face that didn't quite fit the intense way he carried himself. Except it did.

The totality of Bill was almost too much for me to handle.

I still remember the first time he spoke to me.

"*New York Times*, please."

I almost fell off my stool. I stared into his deep brown eyes and felt myself swooning. *Stop it,* I thought. What a dopehead.

"Dollar fifty."

"Thanks."

"You're welcome."

Needless to say, our conversations grew. I kept trying to find ways to facilitate communications. I would vary the music I played in the bookstore to see what he liked or sit reading different magazines and books to see what might catch his interest. I spent hours in the morning deciding what I would wear before going to work. And, I'm embarrassed to admit, the tops may have gotten more snug.

Our first conversation came about because of one of my music selections: B.B. King. Finally. I had been through classical, pop, rock, show tunes, reggae, and soul before I made it to the blues. The blues did it. B.B. did it. I will always thank B.B. King for bringing me and Bill together.

There was something different when he walked in that day. He smiled at me, and his eyes lit up. As usual, I swooned (despite my best efforts).

"You've got B.B. on today," he said.

"Yeah. You like it?"

"I love the blues."

"Yeah? So do I." It wasn't a lie. I did love the blues. I just didn't think he would love the blues. I mean, based on my informal research in the bookstore, the taste of the typical Berkeley-based *New York Times* print reader tended to run more toward classical or jazz or, well, punk.

"Did you know his old band is still playing and is coming to the Bay Area?"

"They are?" Okay, I did know and had been planning to get tickets but hadn't gotten around to it. The more time I laid off from school, the less I tended to get done.

"I was planning to go with some friends. Would you like to join us?"

Would I? Would I? Pow. I could barely contain myself.

"Sure. That sounds like fun." Was I cool or what?

"Okay, well, I'll let you know."

"Okay."

I walked on a cloud the rest of the day. The MAN had asked me out, and while it was not necessarily a date, it was close.

We saw the B.B. King Blues Band at Kimbel's East, one of those great old clubs. Dark, raucous. It was fabulous. The band was fabulous. Bill's friends were fabulous. Bill, naturally, was fabulous. It was one fabulous evening. We went in a group—six of us—two other men and two other women. I kept trying to figure out if he was dating any of the women—or, heck, any of the men—but he didn't seem to be gravitating toward any one of them. All of them were from

Bill's journalism program and had moved to the Bay Area specifically for the graduate program, so seemed to have clustered together out of necessity.

We sat to watch the show. Bill sat next to me. Every once in a while, his thigh would rub up against mine (it was a small place), and the vibrations that went through my body were just incredible. It had been a while since I'd had sex, and I must admit that I was craving it like nobody's business. The blues didn't help. I personally find the blues to be incredibly sensual, and sitting there in the dark with Bill drinking beers and listening to B.B. King's band made me quite toasty.

Then Bill's hand just happened to drop onto my thigh. Oh my god. I would have started hyperventilating if I hadn't swigged my beer and gestured for another. I looked over at Bill. He looked over at me, his deep brown eyes gazing into mine in a way that made me feel he could see into my soul, and I let my hand happen to drop lightly onto his.

The band was playing "Drowning in the Sea of Love," and, man oh man, I was. It was so sensual. Bill's hand began moving in time with the music, and I felt like I might explode at any moment. And then, and then, he kissed me.

We were in the back of the club. In a very dark corner in the back. We were behind his friends, who faced the stage, so no one could see us. Bill leaned over and pressed his lips against mine and wow. Just wow. I wanted him so desperately at that point I didn't know what to do. Or how I could wait. But I did. I just pressed my lips back against his, and the connection was so powerful. Like electricity. It really was a kiss to end all kisses.

"I can't get enough of your love…" *Sing it, B.B. King band,* I thought. And they were. And I was kissing Bill. And he was kissing me. I swear we sat there for hours enjoying the electricity surge our lips were producing, but I know it probably wasn't that long. The set ended. Everyone was clapping. The lights came up. Bill and I pulled apart. He stared into my eyes again with a look that seemed as surprised as I was at the chemical reaction we were producing. His friends turned, and we turned and smiled in an attempt to look oh so chaste and pure. I'm not sure how successful it was.

"Nice set, huh?"

"Yeah. Even without B.B., they put on a great show."

 Later that night Mark, who drove, dropped us off at our cars, which were near the Berkeley campus. The others dispersed, and Bill and I stood next to our cars.

"So," Bill said, "would you like to, uh, go out some time? Maybe to a movie?"

"Sure. When?"

"How about tonight?"

"It's one o'clock in the morning.

"Well, I have Netflix."

"Oh. Netflix." Naturally, I knew what he was asking and, my body still burning from the club, I decided to go along with it. "Sounds like fun."

"Good." Bill beamed. "Why don't you follow me?"

"Great." I crawled into my car and hit my head against the dashboard a couple times to make sure I wasn't dreaming. Nope. No dream.

♡ ♥ ♡

Needless to say, we never got around to watching anything on Netflix. The next day I was at work when he walked up to buy his *New York Times*.

"Well, hello."

Ah. That voice. I could feel myself turning eight shades of scarlet. I turned and there were those eyes again.

"Hi."

"How are you?"

"I'm good," I said. "You?"

"I'm fabulous."

"Fabulous?" He felt fabulous?

"Yeah. Musta been the band."

"You think it was the band?"

"No, not really." And then he smiled. A wicked "baby, it was good" kind of smile. Oh God. Please strike me down at this very moment, and I will die happy, I promise.

"No?" I asked.

"No."

"Well, then, what do you think it was that made you feel so fabulous?"

"I'm not sure, but if you're game, we can try again tonight to figure it out."

"Kind of like an experiment?"

"Yeah. An in-depth experiment."

"In-depth, huh?" I was giving him my best wicked "baby it was good" kind of smile.

"Yeah."

"Sounds good," I said. "I mean... sounds fabulous."

"Great. See you tonight."

He sauntered off with his *New York Times*, and I was left with the most wicked grin that ever existed plastered across my face. Life was good.

That was over five years ago, and the memory still conjured up the same feelings. Oh Bill. No. No Bill. It was Nick what's-his-name. I suddenly realized I had the "baby, it was good" smile plastered on my face while I was walking with Nick what's-his-name across the campus toward Sproul Hall. And he was talking. What was he saying?

"... at the revival house and I thought maybe, if you weren't doing anything, you might want to go and see it."

"What?" What the fuck was he talking about?

"Sabrina."

"Sabrina?"

"The movie. The original. Audrey Hepburn. William Holden. Humphrey Bogart."

"Oh. 'Sabrina.' What about it?"

"It's playing at the Telegraph Friday night. Would you like to see it?"

"With you?"

"Uh, yeah."

"A date?"

"Yeah. I guess you could call it that."

"Huh. Well. Sure. I guess that would be okay."

Nick got this gleeful grin. "Great. I'll give you a call."

I smiled. Actually, I felt pretty good. "Okay."

Nick started off in the opposite direction, leaving me standing next to Sproul Hall. Funny. I was going to say no. I mean, with the War Council and all, I was going to be very busy. But just then, when he asked, I noticed that his blue eyes were really quite blue. Quite lovely, actually. And they were framed by these beautiful lashes. He was actually good looking. Quite good looking. That discovery, coupled with the sexual excitement the memory of meeting Bill had conjured up in me, had me thinking "why the hell not?"

"Sabrina," huh?

Chapter Seven
KATHY

Maggie never knew what hit her. She was preoccupied with the War Council, I'll give her that. Still, she fell for the oldest trick in the book. The ole "I happened to be walking by" ploy. Naturally, it was planned. I knew that Maggie would place the ad in the *Daily Cal* after her two o'clock class, so Nick was strategically placed right outside in the quad. We had to catch her in a position where she wouldn't have too much time to think. I knew Maggie. If we allowed her to think about whether or not she should go out with Nick, she would find eight million reasons why she shouldn't or couldn't go—be it the War Council, her classes, or Bill. Bill. Damn Bill. I must admit that much of my interest in this project lay in helping Maggie get over Bill.

I was also still interested in proving the War Council wouldn't work. In all my years as a counselor, I had never seen evidence that people should coerce other people into commitment.

If the feeling isn't mutual, it just isn't right. I had heard enough horror stories to know.

I was working in the Student Psychological Services department at Berkeley. SPS is a staff of psychiatrists, psychologists, and doctoral candidates who counsel Berkeley students. Apart from the usual stress-related problems of university life, unresolved childhood traumas, and residual assertiveness deficiencies, I spent a lot of time listening to relationship woes. The university environment creates a dating pool that has yet to be rivaled so, naturally, I ended up counseling a lot of students who were particularly unhappy with their relationships. Let's face it: Happy people don't tend to choose psychological services as a place to spend an hour.

The unhappiness among the 20-somethings I saw tended to manifest itself in two basic areas: the person who feels pressured (needs space) and the person who feels insecure (needs love). This is your basic unbalanced love relationship. The person who feels pressured needs space. They do not feel as ardently (or, at times more accurately, possessively) as the insecure person. The insecure person senses this and, seeking validation of love, tries to coerce the pressured person into expressing their feelings more ardently. The pressured person, then, feels more pressure.

In essence, the insecure person desperately needs to hear and feel things the pressured person cannot give, thus forcing the pressured person into a situation where they might lash out or ask for more space or close up. None of these reactions will reassure the insecure person, so they push harder, and ultimately it's a destructive cycle.

As you can probably guess, for most people trapped in this cycle, happiness lies not in the relationship but in themselves. The insecure individual needs to learn to believe in themselves apart from the relationship. And the pressured individual needs to learn to not feel guilty for expressing their own needs and desires. Once these people learn to find the answers within themselves, they are able to move on to find and enjoy healthier relationships.

This is why I hated Maggie's War Council concept so much. It seemed to me that the War Council would only bring more pressure into relationships that were already uneven and pressure filled. What would the War Council do? Coerce one partner into not feeling insecure and another into not feeling pressured? Impossible. To say that love can come through coercion is crazy. Love can grow through time and space and individual growth, but a War Council cannot create these things. Obviously, Maggie felt differently, which is why I sent Nick to track her down in the quad outside the *Daily Californian* offices.

The anti-War Council War Council conspiracy did not stop at Nick and Maggie's rendezvous at the quad. Shoot, by then we had already planned what they would do on their first date—down to the fact that they would go to see *Sabrina*. I had asked Randy and Hallie to be involved in our little project, and it was Randy who suggested *Sabrina* (for reasons that will be explained later).

We had met at my house the evening after the first official War Council meeting on campus. Naturally, I made a little dinner for everyone. Just some sliced heirloom tomatoes in a vinaigrette, marinated butterflied leg of lamb, and scalloped potatoes. Rather civilized for a conspiracy, I suppose, but I didn't see why we couldn't add a little class to the operation.

Brian would never admit it, but I think he was a little put out that Maggie hadn't included him in the War Council. I understood her motives. His research was, admittedly, a little "rat oriented," and we'd been married for so long that he wasn't well versed in dating etiquette. But he was Nick's friend—and my husband—so I included him in our little plot.

Nick, Hallie, Randy, Brian, and I sat around the table conversing and enjoying the dinner. The lamb, by the way, was delicious. I'd had them marinate it at this little store on Union Street. They do such a nice job. After dinner, we would break into our mini-troops to design a strategy for Maggie and Nick. At the moment, though, it felt like any other dinner party.

I looked over at Nick. He was chatting away about surfing the beaches of Brazil. I really did like him. He seemed like such a good fellow and had a real spirit of adventure. I wasn't sure why he wanted to use this War Council idea to get to know Maggie but, for his sake, for Maggie's sake… and mine, I hoped it worked. That might sound strange after having just heard my reasons for wanting to disprove the War Council concept, but I just wanted to show Maggie that love (with someone other than Bill) was possible while hopefully also proving that coercion was not the way to deal with relationships. In order to show Maggie that coercion was wrong, we had to show her what it felt like. Right? I sure hoped so. In the meantime, maybe she would fall in love with Nick.

Maybe I was rationalizing, but I thought we might all come out winners. Nick would get Maggie. Maggie would get Nick. And I would never have to hear about Bill or the War Council again. I sure hoped what I was doing was right as I ran the risk of proving my point while losing my best friend.

After dinner, we split into two groups. The guys interviewed Nick to get an idea of his background and things we could use strategically. Hallie and I worked on an overall game plan. Hallie was the strategist while I provided the details from Maggie's life. On Hallie's suggestion, I had made up two charts. One traced the progression of Bill and Maggie's relationship—from their meeting at the bookstore through the breakup. The other showed Maggie's interests, Bill's interests, and Nick's interests.

Hallie and I analyzed the charts and decided that we should have Nick's interests and the progression of the relationship differ significantly from Bill's. This way we would eliminate the comparison factor. The men Maggie dated after Bill tended to fail because she continually compared them to Bill. The guys, being polite, would ask her what she wanted to do. She would pick something she'd done with Bill. Then she'd feel miserable because she wasn't with Bill and dump the poor guy before he had a chance. Our thinking was: If we take away everything that might remind Maggie of Bill, wouldn't that, in essence, remove the tendency to compare?

The answer—at least in our minds—was yes. So, the first date was designed around two facts. One: Bill was not that into movies. They rarely went out to the movies and never to old movies. So, *Sabrina* would be a surprise—a pleasant surprise, we hoped. Randy had pointed out that *Sabrina* (the original 1954 version) was not only playing soon at the Telegraph but was about a young woman (Audrey Hepburn) who thinks she is in love with William Holden but ends up discovering she really loves his brother Humphrey Bogart. A lot of hidden meaning there, don't you agree? Also, the movie is filled with this wonderful old Edith Piaf song *"La Vie en Rose,"* which is not only incredibly romantic but might remind Maggie of the fact that Nick and Randy sang the song the first night she met him at our dinner party. We needed to build some shared moments.

The second fact we built the date around was that Maggie had the hots for Bill for months before he finally asked her out, and that once they went out, there was little or no "courtship" (for lack of a better word) before they became a couple. It was a one-sided crush, then immediately into lovers. We didn't have the luxury of Maggie actually being infatuated with Nick—after Bill, there were no infatuations—so we had to build that into the relationship. Maggie always seemed to be more comfortable when becoming interested first, so we would manufacture the interest from her side through manipulation.

The way we did that would be to have Nick put off any sort of romantic intentions until we sensed Maggie's interest. They would go out. They would become friends. But he would move very slowly before making any big physical or romantic gestures.

I know it sounds incredibly manipulative, and I kind of hated myself for it. But if you had listened to three years of Bill laments the way I had, you would have resorted to drastic measures, too.

The date went off as planned. Nick told me he took Maggie to see *Sabrina* at the Telegraph.

It was very romantic. They sat in a dark room at close quarters watching a black-and-white film from an era that really knew about romance (according to Randy). Later, they walked through campus and sat at the fountain and looked up at the stars. That was my idea. I knew Maggie had a thing about the campus at night and loved taking walks through it when it was quiet and dark. We all have our little quirks, and that was hers. It was also something she had never done with Bill.

Then, he finished walking her home, kissed her on the cheek, and said good night. No attempts at anything more physical, no mention of another date, and no communication for four days. Maggie was blown away. I know because it was all she could talk about when we met the next week at Café Strada.

"It was the strangest thing," she said.

"What?" I looked as innocent as I could when I inquired.

"Well, we went out. We had a nice time. Really nice time. But then nothing beyond a kiss on the cheek."

"So…"

"So, it's weird, don't you think? And I haven't heard from him since."

"So…"

"So, I don't know." She pondered. "Do you think he's gay?"

I laughed. "Nick? No. From what he has told Brian, I can say with complete certainty he is attracted to women."

"Oh."

"Did you want him to try something?"

"No, of course not. I mean. He's no Bill, right? Still. It was odd..."

Maggie got this far-off quizzical look. Aha! It wasn't logical. Why didn't I think of that to begin with? I guess it didn't matter because it was working. She was definitely intrigued.

Then Nick arrived. It was so perfect you'd have thought we had planned it. And we had.

"Well, hi, Nick," I said.

"Hello ladies. I thought I might find you here."

Nick smiled that twinkling smile of his. I smiled. Maggie smiled. She softened perceptibly as she looked up at Nick and actually seemed pleased to see him.

"Hi," she said.

"Hi," he said.

They locked eyes, and I took that as a sign to make myself scarce. I excused myself to go to the bathroom and peered out from behind the glass to see how it was going. So far so good. I couldn't see if Maggie was turning red or not. She always got flushed when she was excited—or drinking wine—and she wasn't drinking wine. After some meaningless conversation, Nick was going to ask her out again. I saw her nodding. And smiling. Perfect. I was excited—this date was going be even better than the first.

Life was good. Maggie was showing an interest in Nick, and the War Council had not had a single client in the week since Maggie had placed the ad. She was going to have to go out and recruit a test case to make it work. Pah. Impossible. Who would be that desperate?

Chapter Eight
CINDY

The little shit had finally gone too far this time. Just too far. I mean, I had my pride, right? See, I had baked him some brownies. He said he was going to be home studying and sounded sad, so I thought I would cheer him up—especially as he had been studying an awful lot lately. The brownies were going to be a happy surprise, ya know?

I went over to the frat house and walked up to his room on the third floor. I knocked on his door. No answer. I looked in (it was never locked). No Biff. I went downstairs to the fraternity study room. No Biff, but Bunny was there studying with her new boyfriend Kirk. I asked them if they'd seen Biff, and they said no, but then Kirk got a funny look on his face, and as I was leaving, he started whispering something to Bunny. Not that I was paranoid, but I had sensed something was up for awhile. And, okay, maybe that was the real reason for the visit with the brownies.

I walked back through the frat house. From the outside, it was this beautiful old mansion. Like, you'd picture some old fart living there in immense wealth and culture. But inside, it always looked as if a bomb had hit. There was practically no furniture and what they had was ratty and disgusting. Plus, the floor was always sticky from all the beer that had spilled over the years.

I remembered Biff telling me about one of their initiation rituals. He said the older members filled the basement with beer and made the pledges wear helmets and then go sliding across the floor like a slip 'n' slide before banging into the wall. And some of the pledges had gotten sick so they were really sliding across a beer-and-vomit-soaked floor before crashing into a brick wall. Biff said it was rad, and I remembered thinking that I would never understand boys.

I checked the rec room. Also sticky and still no Biff. Kevin was there. Kevin was Biff's roommate and really sweet. I had always kind of liked Kevin. He had curly blond hair and was really easy to talk to. If I hadn't thought I'd be spending the rest of my life with Biff, I might have liked Kevin, you know, that way. The thing is, he really seemed to like me, too, and sometimes got weird about Biff and the way he treated me. Not around Biff, though. They were buds. That's why it was sometimes kind of weird how he tried to, in secret, tell me to take care of myself when it came to Biff. I always told him about Biff's sweet side and that he wasn't really the macho dude he pretended to be, that it really was a cover for the other guys, and that he didn't know Biff the way I did. But Kevin kept trying to protect me, like a big brother would.

Actually, he was my big brother. The fraternity had this, like little-sister thing where we girls would come to a party and the guys chose some of us to be "little sisters." Naturally, because I was Biff's girlfriend, I got picked.

I think you can see now just how much Biff's loving me did for my life. Anyway, it was really cool. Each girl then got paired with a guy—a "bro." That's what they all called each other. In the sorority, we were "sisters," and in the fraternity, they were "brothers." I always thought it was cool because I never had a big family, and now I had all these brothers and sisters.

So, what happens with a big brother is you do nice things for the guy you're paired with. I would clean Kevin's room, which was kind of like cleaning Biff's room, too (funny, huh?), bring him cookies, and stuff. You know. Do nice things for him. And he did nice things for me. Took me for ice cream. Helped me with my studies. Sometimes it seemed like I spent more time with Kevin than I did with Biff.

You see, Biff was really busy now that he was a senior. He studied a lot and said I was too much of a distraction to study around, so he mostly studied by himself. And by distraction, I mean that whenever Biff was around me, he'd want to, you know, have sex. Biff always wanted sex. Not that I minded. I liked it, too, and it was nice to be wanted like that. Only, it would have been nice to have him enjoy being around me in other ways, too, you know? Like Kevin could be around me and do fun things with me that didn't involve sex, so why couldn't Biff?

I know it's different because Biff loved me. But still. And when I say Biff wanted it all the time, I mean all the time. We'd be at a party, and he'd want a quickie in the bathroom or a closet. We were once at a party at his parents' house, and he said he wanted to show me a book upstairs in his room, and we ended up doing it while his mom was serving martinis and pigs-in-a-blankets to the guests downstairs. Geez, I was so embarrassed, especially as it seemed like everyone knew when we got back downstairs. We got these looks. Actually, I got the looks. In Biff's mom's eyes, he could do no wrong. I was the "influence."

Still, Biff loved me. I mean, how could a guy want someone as much as Biff wanted me and not love me? And I loved him. I would dream about becoming Mrs. Robert Billingsley V. My friends—oops, sisters—and I would plan our weddings all the time. We would pick our bridesmaids, what colors we'd choose, where it would be, and what our husbands would look like. Naturally, I always pictured Biff. He was the only guy I'd ever been with, and he was so perfect—why wouldn't I want to spend the rest of my life with him? I mean, okay, there were times he was kind of a jerk—like when he would stand me up or forget to call or, like now, just disappear. And he sure seemed to be studying an awful lot.

"He's not studying," Kevin said.

"What do you mean he's not studying?" I looked at Kevin like he was nuts. Well, he was. Biff was studying.

"He's not studying."

"Then where is he?"

"I'd rather not say."

"Why not?"

"Because I'm trapped in a no-win situation here," said Kevin.

"What do you mean?"

"I tell you and Biff hates me. I have to live with the guy, remember? But if I don't tell you, then you hate me. I don't want you to hate me, Cindy."

Kevin smiled one of his nice, if rueful, smiles. He was so sweet. Why couldn't Biff be more like him?

"Please tell me, Kevin." I did my best to look miserable. And vulnerable. And sexy. It was the look that always made Biff crazy for me.

"He's at the Kingfish," he said.

"The Kingfish?" It took a moment to sink in. And then it did. All my worst fears were coming true. That fuckface asshole. Studying? Ha! I would show him studying, the little weasel. Kevin got this shocked look on his face, and I realized I was letting my emotions show on my face. I put the vulnerable look back on.

"Thanks, Kevin. Here, have some brownies."

I ran out of that dump they called a fraternity house and over to the Kingfish. The Kingfish was this dive bar where the fraternity guys went to get wasted and hook up with girls (and not necessarily in that order). Studying. Ha!

I walked through the doors and practically choked from the smell of sweat and beer and grease. Where was that son-of-a-bitch? Huh? I would find him if it was the last thing I ever did. And I would make him squirm.

Then I saw him—with his arms draped around that what's-er-name. What a sleaze bucket she was. His little sister. Not his real littler sister, you know: his fucking fraternity little sister. I remember thinking she was a little slut when I first saw her bringing cookies and stuff to Biff. Like she laced her brownies with marijuana and thought she was *so* clever. Her hair was this teased bleached puff, she wore way too much make-up, and I remember wondering why Biff picked this obvious sleaze to be his little sister. Now I knew: So he could screw her when my back was turned. Studying, ha!

Biff saw me and waved me over. Like he wasn't even embarrassed about lying to me and cheating on me. Asshole.

"Hey, baby, what's up?" said Biff. "You remember Kitty."

Kitty. What kind of stupid ass name is that?

Biff probably thought I wasn't going to get angry. Well, this time he had gone too far. I was not going to back down and take it anymore.

94

"Biff," I said quietly. "I would like to have a word with you, if you could possibly remove yourself from ole Kitty here."

"Sure, babe. Don't have a coronary."

"Oh, heh heh, don't worry," said Kitty. "I have to go to the little girl's room anyway."

The sleaze spoke. Little girl's room. What did Biff see in this piece of trash? She walked off— or, should I say, wriggled off as it was virtually impossible to actually walk in the dress she had shellacked onto her body.

"So, what's up?"

"Biff, you told me you were studying. You lied to me. And now I find you here with your arms all over this hussy, and all you can say to me is 'what's up'?"

"Meow. Let's not be so possessive here."

"Possessive? Possessive? What am I sup-posed to think about what is going on here, Biff? I mean, we are pinned, right?"

"Sure, but come on! That was a joke. Listen, baby, I am 22 years old, and if you think I'm ready to settle down with one girl, you're crazy."

"Crazy? Crazy?" I couldn't believe what I was hearing. Where was my sweet sensitive Biff who I loved more than life itself? Who was this asshole? What had happened to the Biff who brought me champagne and listened to my plans and said he wanted to spend his life with me?

"I've been meaning to tell you," he said.

"Tell me what?"

"I'm just kind of needing some space right now, that's all."

"Space?"

"Yeah, I'm getting these urges."

"Urges?"

"Yeah, physical urges. Like to be with other girls. It has nothing to do with you."

I thought my head was going to explode. "It doesn't?"

"No. You're my baby. My girlfriend. I want to stay with you and maybe someday we can, you know, be together together. But right now, I kind of want to play the field. See what's out there. Be wild. You know?"

I was shaking. "No, I don't."

"See. You just don't understand what it's like to be a guy. We have to be wild every once in a while. It's just physical, babe."

"I am not your babe."

"Oh, come on now. Don't get excited," he said.

"You tell me you are fucking other women, but it's 'just physical' and I shouldn't get excited?" My voice was getting a little loud now, but I didn't care. Biff looked freaked. I was embarrassing him in "his bar" but tough, asshole.

"Calm down, Cindy. See, that's why I told you I was studying. I knew you wouldn't understand, and I didn't want to hurt your feelings."

"So, you lied to me?"

"Well, yeah. It was for the best. I mean, look at your reaction."

He was talking to me like I was a child. Like a fucking child.

"Fuck you, Biff the fucking fifth."

"Come on, babe."

And then I started crying. Damn, I hated that. Whenever I got mad, really mad, I started to cry. It was so horrible. How can you get mad at people if every time you do you start to cry?

Biff's eyes darted around to see if anyone he knew was watching us. The little asshole was worried about his image as my heart was breaking. I looked over and saw the sleaze leave the restroom. She smirked at the little scene I was causing. I couldn't handle it anymore, so I broke away from Biff and ran outside.

I stood near the alley outside the bar and thought I was going to throw up. I kept picturing the two of them fucking. I pictured Biff doing to the sleaze all the things he had done to me— all the personal, private, intimate things we did together. The things that bonded us as a couple. That we shared. The things that made me feel beautiful and special.

Special. Ha! I'm sure they had a big laugh over that one.

I felt cheap. I felt used. All I kept seeing was Biff with the shellacked dress who put pot in his brownies. And who else? What other sleaze had he screwed before coming to visit me at the sorority house?

And then I did throw up.

After I threw up, I noticed there was someone standing beside me and a packet of Kleenex being offered. I took one and then saw who it was doing the offering: Oh shit, it was a professor. I'm puking on the sidewalk outside the Kingfish, and a professor is watching me.

"Sorry," I mumbled.

"Don't worry about it." She smiled at me. She was one of the younger faculty members and had black hair and these really piercing green eyes. I recognized her but couldn't place the face yet—maybe I'd had one of her courses back when I was a freshman.

"Listen," she continued. "I couldn't help but notice that you were in a bit of distress in there. Maybe I can help?"

"Help?"

"Yeah. You want to go and get a cup of coffee? The Edible Complex is only a half a block away."

It was all kind of weird. But she did look nice, like maybe she understood. And I definitely needed someone to talk to. She was a professor, right, so she had to be smart. What did I have to lose?

Chapter Nine
MONIQUE

Maggie came to see me in my office on campus. She was bubbling full of excitement. Said she'd found our first client. Someone she'd pounced on while hanging out at the Kingfish. Interesting methodology, but we did have our first client. I was glad. The semester was proving to be truly dull. Duller than usual. The students were all dolts with not an inspired thinker in the bunch. It didn't help I had been teaching the same course for the third semester in a row. Truly dull. And the topic of the paper I was working on was not stimulating me as it once had.

We'd also had more than our fair share of rain in the Bay Area. It was April, and the endless drizzle-filled cloudy days were beginning to get to me. Normally I enjoy the rain and the angst that comes with it but this, this was a bit much. The gray days just seemed to stretch on and on.

For the first time in I don't know how many years, I was ready for spring. Real spring, not the calendar-induced variety. Not that I'm into premonitions or any of that New Age woo-woo stuff, but I couldn't help but feel that something was about to happen and that it would come with the spring. The true spring. With blue skies and breezy days and purple blossoms blooming on the jacaranda. But, no, spring was not in the air. Not yet.

The young woman Maggie acquired as our first client sounded a bit pedestrian, but definitely in need of aid. I had seen the type all too often on the Berkeley campus: Still trapped in delusions of Cinderella and the prince on the white horse and men providing all the answers to her problems. No need to find herself or a life for herself except as Mrs. Whatever. Poor child, she could definitely use some work.

The prick who was her boyfriend was another matter. Maggie mentioned his name and it sounded familiar, so I looked on my roster and discovered he had been one of my students a previous semester. One of the neofascists that followed me around like lost puppies and then called me Professor Hard Ass behind my back. Yes, I knew they called me that and that I represented some sort of fantasy conquest in their pea brains. It would be enjoyable to skewer one of the wolf pack.

Men. I've always had problems with men. My politics don't endear me to a large swath of the male population. Not that I respect most of them anyway, with their need to uphold an archaic image. Not that many women are any better in their participation in perpetuating the patriarchal order. So many reward the posturing and revel in their victimhood. All in all, it's such a tedious exercise.

All things considered, though, I enjoy men. Quality men. Unfortunately, they are frightfully few in number, especially in the states. They run for the hills when presented with a woman who has something to say—something I didn't find as much when I did my graduate work in Paris and found any number of men with an affinity for both my intellect and my body.

My fondness for foreign cultures—and the ability to disappear on campus—was the reason I spent much of my time between classes and office hours at the University International House. The I-House had a very nice café that overlooked Campus Avenue and was my secret haven with the foreign voices surrounding me blending together to allow me to muse uninterrupted.

I had been sitting at the I-House since seeing Maggie on campus and, naturally, pondering the nature of love and relationships. Ever since Maggie first approached me with the War Council project, I had been focused on an examination of the dilemmas of relationships in the post-millennial era. Now that we had a client, some of my theories could be put into practice.

I was mid-muse when HE came in. Mike, the lout—and a perfect illustration of the flaws in the American male, I might add.

"Well, hey, if it ain't my War Council comrade."

Oh no, he spotted me. What was he doing here? This was my secret enclave. Why wasn't he with the pretentious people-watching crowd at Café Strada? I asked him.

"Strada? Yuckola. Not into Strada. That cappuccino stuff is for the birds. This place has beer. Good beer. It's also where I come to meet with some of my players. A lot of them are Aussies and live here at the I-House. Waiting for one of them now. Mind if I pull up a chair?"

"Must you?"

"Come on, cookie. Loosen up. We're on the same team now, remember?"

"Don't call me cookie," I said. "I am not your cookie."

"Yeah, gotcha, *Professor* DeVillier. Or Professor Hard Ass, as the players call ya. Did you know that?"

"I have heard the moniker before."

"Woo. Touchy."

I couldn't figure out why he felt such a need to keep this macho dude act up. Then it dawned on me. "You really can't help it, can you?"

"Can't help what?"

"Being a dickhead."

"A dickhead?" He burst out laughing, a big ridiculously boisterous laugh.

"Yes, a dickhead," I said. "Do you practice?"

"Being a dickhead?" He burst out laughing again.

"What?" He was really annoying me now. Before he answered, he stared me straight in the eye.

"It's just that I didn't think 'dickhead' was in your vocabulary. Is that the official academic term?"

"I'm just trying to relate to you on your level." I stared back. Why not?

"Nah, that's not it," he said.

"Oh, and what is?"

"I'll just bet there's a fun broad inside all that posturing."

"Me posturing? *Me* posturing?"

"Keep going, cookie. Loving it."

"Don't 'cookie' me. Please leave."

"I'm getting to you."

"Oh, please, you are not getting to me. You're bugging the hell out of me."

"More vocabulary amendments!"

"Don't you have a Neanderthal to meet?"

"A Neanderthal?"

"You know, one of those sports types you coach."

"You think all male sports types are Neanderthals? Isn't that gender stereotyping, professor?"

Okay, he got me. I set myself up and, for the first time I noticed that, actually, Mike was somewhat aesthetically pleasing—in an athletic sort of way. A bit on the stocky side and not all that tall, but he was built. I liked that. He had a nice chest. The kind of chest that could really envelop you. One of the problems with all those sensual Europeans who respected my intelligence was that they were all so damn scrawny.

So, Mike wasn't bad looking. And he had this funny hair that seemed to spike out in all directions. Endearing, it was. That wasn't the problem. The problem was, and let's be frank about it, the problem was that the minute he opened his mouth, all the appeal vanished.

MIKE

I was getting to her. Getting through the ice facade she presented to the world. She wasn't a bad broad. Had a lot of spunk. And definitely not bad to look at. Actually pretty damn perfect in the looks department: The kind of eyes they model contact lenses on except hers are real, and okay, she had a bod to die for.

So, it was the bod I noticed first. Sue me; I'm a dude. She was tall and the type of gal who wore turtleneck shirts, baggy blazers, and slacks, but there was no hiding what was underneath, and it was spectacular (if you know what I mean). And she always wore this bright red lipstick. Always felt like a bit of an anomaly from what I heard of her "hard-ass" reputation—but, heck, I guess that's what they fought for, right? I don't know.

Still, I did have fun baiting her, you know? I just kept wondering if there was something there beneath her hard-ass exterior. At least she had a mind. So many of the babes I meet are a big zero in the brains department. I liked a little challenge. I mean, I was the only boy in a family of six kids, so teasing girls was my specialty. They'd get so mad and scream and squeal. Guys don't do that. They hit. Not nearly as much fun.

She didn't know how to answer that last one. Gender stereotyping was one of her topics. I knew because I had looked up some of her books and articles on the Internet after meeting her at Kathy's dinner party. She was actually a damn good writer. I sent one of the articles—on equality in pay for services—to my sister who's a broker on Wall Street. Seems like a no-brainer to me: If a woman does equal work, she deserves equal pay. I'm all for that.

"Did you hear Maggie found a client for the War Council?"

Oh good. She'd stopped pouting and decided to speak to me. I hadn't heard about the client, so Monique told me what she knew.

"Guy sounds like a prick."

Monique looked surprised. "You think he sounds like a prick?"

"Any dude that cheats on his woman is a prick. If he was at all honorable, he would have broken up with her before slamming the babes."

"And here I thought maybe you had an ounce of decency."

"What?"

"'Slamming babes?' That is so degrading."

"Why? I'm not talking about you."

"But you are talking about my sex."

"Well, you could say you slammed some dudes."

"But I wouldn't."

"Why not?"

"Because it degrades the whole act of sex."

"Hey, there are two kinds of sex. They require two kinds of action verbs. Sport sex—the variety pricks like this Biff dude are into—uses words like slamming, bopping, humping, doing, hooking up, whatever. Sex that expresses love is a completely different matter."

I looked at her eyes. She seemed surprised. I wasn't sure if it was a delighted sort of surprise or a disgusted sort of surprise. Either way, those amazing eyes just shone.

MONIQUE

That last one really surprised me. The fact that the lout even thought about love—or that sex differed when a person was expressing love—astonished me. I mean, the way he spoke, the way he carried himself and his mannerisms suggested more of a Neanderthal quality.

Could I be wrong about him? Could there be a sensitive caring individual in there? Could the upcoming spring bring out a depth I could not have imagined?

I looked over at his eyes, at the hair that couldn't quite decide where to fall, at the powerful chest just begging to be hugged. Then he belched, grinned, took a swig of his beer, and it all disappeared. Neanderthal.

Chapter Ten

NICK

Spring had sprung. For the first time in what seemed like months, the clouds began to part, and the sun began to shine. The change in the mood on campus was remarkable. Suddenly, there were people everywhere. I wondered where all these people had hidden themselves throughout the rainy winter and early spring. They also carried with them a new attitude. I saw love blossoming all over campus. Maybe it was the jacaranda trees beginning to blossom their brilliant purple. Maybe it was just my mood. Love was hopefully about to blossom for me. The time had come to ask Maggie out again. I found her in her office.

"We have our first client," she said.

"I heard. Congratulations! How would you like to go out with me to celebrate?"

I looked into her green eyes and (internally I hoped) sighed. She was beautiful, and I was again struck by how manipulative this all was.

The AWAC (what we started calling the Anti-WAr-Council War Council) had timed my asking her out for this date to coincide with the War Council's first client. The reasoning was that Maggie would be on a high, and that would be the best time to pounce.

"I'd like that," she said.

She smiled. Maggie smiled. She smiled at me. Maggie wanted to go out with me. Okay, the plan was working. The clouds were parting, the trees were blossoming, and the plan was working. Hello spring!

"Great," I said. "How about if I pick you up around 8?"

"Great."

I left her office walking on air. So what if the events of the last few weeks had been planned by a group? So what if it was a bit calculating? So what if I already knew more background on Maggie than I had my last two girlfriends? It was working! The pragmatist in me was happy.

It's not that I wasn't a little wary of our methods. I was. But it seemed to me that most relationships have their share of manipulation and game playing—especially in the early stages and these days when Google and social media searches are so easy—so why not do it in an organized way with people who could help point me to the rules of the game? What was wrong with a little research?

Besides, it was Maggie's idea. Her concept. We were just playing by her rules.

We. I'll admit that was the odd part. It wasn't just me and Maggie. It was me and Kathy and Brian and Randy and Hallie and Maggie. I didn't really mind having a team on my side. Maybe it's because I grew up playing sports. I mean, the concept is the same, right? Two heads are better than one. A group working toward a common goal. Learn the rules and win the game.

Again, I figured these were all Maggie's concepts, and I was just playing by her rules. Kind of.

It's not that I feel that I have to justify myself, but I wasn't going to do anything that was against my nature. I was never going to lie. I wanted Maggie to get to know *me*, not a fabricated image. We were just formulating that image in the best light and at the appropriate time. What was so wrong with that?

Like I said, the pragmatist in me was pleased. My romantic side? Well, I tried to make room for that within the parameters of the plan. And I did.

Our second date had been even better than the first. Well, it started off that way at least. That was when we (the AWAC) learned how important timing was to our plan. No one had factored in the fact that Maggie would be too preoccupied by the War Council to think about herself or romance until she had her first client.

We had gone to the Kingfish for dinner. The Kingfish is a Berkeley institution: more dive bar than English pub but an English pub nonetheless. I wasn't sure why Maggie was so bent on going there, but she was.

After we got there, I learned the answer. The place was filled with students. Students mingling, students drinking, students looking for other students to "spend the evening with" (if you get my drift). Lots of couples or those intent on coupling.

Research. Maggie was doing War Council research on our date.

We were there on a Thursday night. It had been arranged that we make the date very casual. Build on the friendship, Kathy said. So we did. Thursday night is very casual, very friendly. Friday and Saturday nights have a distinction as "date" nights and that leads to increased expectations as to whether or not the twosome will be sleeping together at the end of the date, so by asking someone out for a Friday or Saturday night, the expectation is that you are interested in that party romantically. That was Kathy's take, but I will admit that, although I hadn't thought about it, I had rarely asked a woman out on a Friday or Saturday unless I was seriously considering a relationship with her—or, at least, considering making a move.

With Maggie, I was ready to make my move the moment I met her but was holding back in honor of the plan. From what Kathy told us, Maggie hated pressure. Hated the pressure of having someone want her before she wanted him. I could respect that (I suppose), which is why I waited.

If you want to know the truth, it was killing me, but again, the pragmatist in me accepted my fate.

Although my ego was a bit bruised that Maggie was more intent on watching the goings-on at the Kingfish than in getting to know me better, I held back. *Build on the friendship,* I said to myself. Build on the friendship. I held onto those words and was patient and under-standing and friendly. And, I have to admit, the goings-on were quite interesting that night.

Around 10 o'clock, a perky-looking coed came bursting through the doors. She marched right over to a snotty-looking prepster who was seemingly suctioned onto a (to be kind) rather provocatively dressed gal. The provoca-tively dressed gal excused herself and left for the ladies' room while the coed and preppy got into a rather heated discussion. Then the coed started crying and ran out the door.

Maggie got this possessed look on her, and I knew the date was over.

"Listen, Nick. I gotta run. I think this is it. I may be back, but I can't promise, okay? I really had fun. Really I did. And I'd like to do this again, but I have to go. Sorry."

And with that, Maggie was gone. Although the evening was shot, I somehow knew we would have another chance. Timing: Its importance in a relationship cannot be underestimated. And now, the timing was right on. Actually, the AWAC was overjoyed that Maggie had found the War Council client while with me. "Positive association as reinforcement" Kathy called it. Psychological mumbo-jumbo but I knew what she meant. I could tell from the way Maggie looked at me in her office that she definitely associated my presence with good feelings. She appreciated my understanding about her abrupt departure the night before, and now we would have a chance to celebrate. With the friendship built, it was time for romance.

♡ ♥ ♡

I took Maggie to the Rio Dio. The Rio Dio is a club in San Francisco that features Brazilian music—the most sensuous music invented by man (in my personal opinion). Okay, so I was ready to push things a little.

What I really wanted was for Maggie to be as crazy for me as I was for her. That was why I had been so patient and was still being patient and would be patient until it happened, so help me God.

Kathy had told the AWAC about Maggie falling for Bill over B.B. King music. We all felt that music had a special effect on her—an erotic effect, if you will—but that we needed to provide a difference. Maggie associated the blues with Bill. We (I) wanted her to associate the exotic rhythms of Brazil with me. I had developed a love of Brazilian music during my Latin American Studies days. The sensual rhythms had really helped rid me of my WASP reserve, and we (again, I) hoped they would do the same for Maggie.

Not that Maggie was reserved. Maggie had an exuberance and passion for life that translated into seemingly boundless energy. But she also had an emotional aloofness that made it difficult to really get to know her. Her passion and exuberance were funneled into things she could make logical. That damned logic was blocking me from getting to the warm, passionate Maggie I knew existed deep inside. Music had unlocked that passion once. I had to hope it would do so again.

The Rio Dio was packed. It was a Friday night (yes, Friday night!), after all. Friday night at the Rio Dio was locals night. Saturdays and Sundays were for tourists, but Fridays found the Brazilians and other South American natives who lived in the Bay Area congregating at the Rio Dio. The club was located in a big old warehouse in San Francisco's Mission district. It had been converted into a club about ten years earlier and, at one time, had a neon sign out front that said "Rio de Janeiro" but enough lights had burnt out that now it just said Rio d- –i-o. The name stuck, and the owners never changed the lights.

We walked in and the place was already pulsating with the sounds of Spanish, Portuguese, and their various dialects, bringing up memories of my days on the beaches of Rio. What a time that was. I remembered a concert held on the beach in Copacabana where I drank cachaca and found myself dancing in a conga line that snaked the entire length of the boardwalk.

The music at the Rio Dio sounded familiar, so I looked up to see who the singer was. It was Jorge Ben. Kismet. Jorge Ben was the Brazilian singer performing at the concert on the Copacabana. I knew he could provide the magic I needed for this evening with Maggie.

We made our way up to the bar.

"Two cachacas, please."

The bartender nodded and began to mix the drinks.

"What's a cachaca?" Maggie asked.

"It is THE Brazilian drink."

"Well, then I suppose we MUST have it."

She smiled. Her eyes roamed the club. The colorful dancers, colorful accents, and colorful music were mirrored in her eyes as she looked around and then looked back at me.

"This place is great."

"Yeah, I know."

"You come here a lot?"

I nodded. "When I can."

I was suddenly grabbed from behind and pulled into a bear hug. "Nick! Nick! *Boa noite! Come vai?*"

"Mino! *Vou bem. Obligado. E voce?*"

"*Bem...*"

I put my hand up to stop Mino. It would be rude to continue to speak Portuguese when Maggie didn't understand the language. As you've probably guessed, Mino was Brazilian.

He was also one of my oldest friends in the Bay Area. We met when I was doing my field study at the University of Sao Paolo, and now he was in San Francisco getting a law degree.

"Mino, this is Maggie. Maggie, Mino."

Maggie and Mino shook hands while I paid for the drinks, which by now had appeared at the bar. I handed Maggie her drink and stood behind her as she listened to my gregarious friend regale her with stories about our days in Brazil. I silently signaled to Mino that, yes, this was the woman I was interested in and, yes, I wanted to spend some time with her—alone. Mino, being Latin and well versed in the ways of love, nodded and, without missing a beat, finished his story, bid his farewell, and returned to his group.

"Nice guy," said Maggie as she sipped from her drink.

"One of the best. So, would you care to dance? We are here to celebrate, are we not?"

"That we are."

Maggie smiled and finished her drink, and we found our place among the bodies celebrating on the floor. They were celebrating life. Maggie was celebrating the War Council. And I was celebrating Maggie. I was happy to learn that she was a natural dancer. She learned the samba steps quickly and was soon moving gracefully in—and out of—my arms. She seemed to let go, her long black hair and multi-colored skirt swinging around her as she danced. Soon, she became part of the celebration of life that was occurring on the dance floor.

I lost myself watching Maggie amid the colorful dancers and sensual rhythms, watching her green eyes blaze with passion as she moved about the floor and watching the walls that protected her soul fall around her. All the plans, all the waiting, all the frustration of the past few weeks faded into memory as I realized I was falling in love with the vision that was dancing before me.

Chapter Eleven
MAGGIE

Well, I gotta tell you, I was confused. It was just not logical. I was sitting in my War Council offices waiting for the others to arrive. This was our big moment. We were about to make it happen. I was finally reaching my goal—and all I could think about was HIM. And, surprisingly enough, this time the "him" was not Bill, it was Nick.

We'd gone dancing. I love to dance. Dancing is one of the few things in life that allows me to really let go. My overly active brain cells tend to inhibit pure unadulterated feeling from coming out in most aspects of my life. But dancing allows me to really let go and just live without thinking too much.

So, I danced—we danced. And, I have to admit, I got a little wild—I don't know if it was the drink or the music or Nick or what. I was drinking this Brazilian concoction called cachaca. Whatever it was, it tasted good and made me feel good, and loose, and in the mood to groove. Ha. Sorry about that.

Nick had taken me to this great club, a Brazilian club. Funny, I had lived in the Bay Area my whole life and never knew it was there. I felt as though I had been transported to another world—a wild and reckless and carefree world. I became wild and reckless and carefree and left good ole logical, analytical Maggie behind in Berkeley. I hadn't felt so free or, really, sexy in a long time. Really, I hadn't felt like this since… Bill and the blues club.

Not that Nick was anything like Bill. Not that I even knew Nick all that well. He was still somewhat of a mystery to me—an intriguing mystery but a mystery nonetheless. It was funny how he seemed to get better looking the more I got to know him. Also funny how he seemed to understand me SO well and just how good it felt to spend time with him. I hadn't felt a connection like this since… Bill.

Not that Nick was anything like Bill. They didn't look alike at all. Okay, so they both had brown hair, but that's where the similarities ended. Bill's looks—at least to me—were more dramatic looking while Nick's were more, you know, pedestrian. I don't mean he wasn't good looking. He was. It's just that Bill really stood out in a crowd. Nick was the crowd. Not really. But you know what I mean, right? In a crowd, Nick might blend in. It's when you got close that you realized just how exceptional looking he really was.

Especially his eyes. Nick had incredible eyes. Bill had deep brown eyes. Nick's were blue. Bill's eyes were warm brown pools in which I was allowed to lose myself, in which I felt loved, in which I felt safe. Nick's eyes, on the other hand, were this piercing blue. Not as warm, but more penetrating—like they could see right through me into my soul, a soul that hadn't been opened up like that since… Bill.

I gotta say, it scared the shit out of me. I mean, I didn't have time for this—for love. I couldn't lose myself in another person. Not now.

Now many may argue that you don't lose yourself in love and, to that, I answer: Bullshit. That was not my experience. Love removes all level-headed and logical responses, which is why the War Council was so important—and, in a way, why I had been holding onto Bill.

I knew I wasn't holding onto the real Bill, the everyday boyfriend, by thinking about him or that I might still have a future with him. I wasn't that deluded, and naturally, I had Kathy telling me daily that what I was holding onto wasn't real. I knew I was holding onto a fantasy. That's what I liked about it. Whenever I was depressed or lonely or out with a real drip, I could conjure up all the great feelings of being loved and understood. And I could do it without the risk of losing myself again or feeling the pain that came with his departure.

I had never felt pain like the pain I felt when Bill left—a deep searing pain that ripped at my insides. I felt like a gutted fish, my insides spilling out all over the rug as Bill sat telling me it was over. That we could be friends, but we weren't together anymore. As if, poof, that magical wonderful connection we had never existed.

I'm still not sure if it helped that I was older. Still not sure if it helped or hurt my recovery. People say that pain makes us stronger, but does that mean it makes us any better? I had been so open, so trusting, so guileless, and I fell in love without any barriers protecting my soul. It never occurred to me to protect myself. It never occurred to me that Bill wouldn't love me forever. It all seemed so natural, so right, so logical.

My entire belief system was shot. My whole life I had waited to fall in love, to meet the person who would love me and understand me and help me to face the insanity that is daily life. I met him. He was beautiful. He loved me. And he left. I gave him my soul. And he left.

And now, after years of protecting myself, of making my life—me—whole again, I found myself feeling things for this blue-eyed stranger dancing before me. I was opening up. I was feeling. I was living life again. Could I handle it? Was I ready? I didn't want to live the rest of my life protecting myself from any real feeling. And I was finally beginning to accept the fact that Bill wasn't returning to me. So, was this man with the piercing blue eyes the one who could help me to open up and feel again? Maybe it was time to try.

We were having a great time dancing to the Brazilian music. Several times he took me into his arms, and I felt that surge of electricity that signals physical chemistry. Damn chemistry! At once the most wondrous and most maddening force in nature.

After the concert, we went out to the Marina Green, a pocket of beach that looks out at Alcatraz. Still buzzing from the cachaca concoctions (at least I was), we walked along the water and talked and talked. He took my hand. I felt like a school girl, all happy and giddy and amazed that life was beginning for me again.

We stopped at a deserted pier, and he took me into his arms and kissed me. Our first real kiss. Talk about your energy surges. It was simply wondrous. A wondrous kiss. I opened my eyes, and there they were again—those beautiful baby blues looking through me and filling my insides with an incredible warmth. I felt safe. I felt protected. And I felt a need to be with him, you know, really with him (in the biblical sense).

Soon we were lying on his couch kissing and fondling, and I was happy. I wasn't feeling any fear; I just felt good. Like, yes, here we go. We're feeling again. We're feeling again. I could love again. It was possible. I could let Bill go and actually love again. We were listening to Edith Piaf again—the music from the movie we'd seen—some plaintive old love song. It was very romantic, but I have to admit I was curious, so I asked, "What's with the Piaf?"

"What about it?"

"I don't know. It's a little odd for a modern kinda guy like yourself to be listening to Edith Piaf."

He began nibbling on my ear. Oooh. I was such a sucker for that. Then he started with this crazy French accent.

"Ah, mon petite Maggie. Ze music, she is for you. Piaf sings of l'amour. Is romantic, no?"

"I suppose." Okay, so I was playing coy.

"Look how she helped bring romance to Sabrina."

I smiled. His accent was pretty good. Must be all that French lit. Still, I wanted to remind him of all that was good in the states, and my hand looked for the spot that would do it.

"Sabrina, huh? So, Nick, does that make you William Holden?"

He moaned. I'd found the spot.

"I'm hoping that I'm Humphrey Bogart."

"You are, are you?"

My lips continued their way around his face, and his words were becoming more labored.

"Of course I am. Bogey gets the girl, right?"

"He does, but he had to move to Paris to do it."

The lips moved, the hand moved, he was barely whispering now.

"Well, luckily, I am going to be living in Paris."

What? Paris? That's 5,000 miles away. The hand withdrew.

"Oh really? When?" I asked.

"In the fall."

"The fall?" The lips withdrew.

"Yeah."

"For how long?"

"For a year."

A year? A year? The gutted fish feeling returned. I was starting to fall in love with another man who was going to leave me. I couldn't go through that again. I couldn't go through the hurt, the pain, or the suffering of being left. I wanted to be with someone who wanted to be with me, dammit, not someone who would suck the love and life out of me and then leave.

I could feel myself pulling away from him. I couldn't look into those eyes that had pierced my soul. The warm feelings disappeared and the electrical charge that had attracted me now jolted me and made me want out of the room—fast.

"What's wrong?"

"I can't handle this," I said.

"What?"

"I can't handle starting something with you, Nick."

"Why?"

"You're leaving."

"In five months."

"Well, it's too much for me. I can't start something with you knowing it's going to end in five months. I'm not built that way. Sorry."

I grabbed my things and got out of there as quickly as I could. I couldn't believe how close I had come to totally losing myself. Really succumbing. I made it out of there without losing my heart. Whew, right? Wrong. What lingered was not a feeling of relief or safety. Instead it was an image: an image of Nick's blue eyes as he said good-bye. The eyes that looked so lost, so disappointed, and just so sad.

♡ ♥ ♡

My thoughts were interrupted by the arrival of my troops. Great. The War Council would help me out of my confused state, keep me busy, and keep that final image of Nick's somber eyes out of my mind. Sure. That would work.

"General Maggie, what's shakin'?"

Mike was the first to arrive and made a big show of saluting. That made me smile. I needed to smile.

"Captain Mike, glad you could make it."

"Hard ass here yet?"

"I'm right behind you, Neanderthal."

"Monique, babycakes, how's it hanging?"

I cringed, but Monique took it in stride. "Fine, toots." With that, she clapped Mike on the butt and commented, "Yeow, firm buns."

She then grinned, winked at me, turned, took a seat, and crossed her legs without missing a beat. Mike was shocked. I was shocked, too, but tried not to look like I had enjoyed the exchange as much as I did.

Before either of us could comment, Kathy, Randy, and Hallie walked through the door. They were talking about the sunny day. I guess the sun was out—so what? It was spring after all, why shouldn't the sun be shining?

"Okay, let's get to work." I attempted to take control while they took their seats.

"Yes, Teach," Kathy said in a snarky tone.

Had to cause trouble. Jealous of the success, I suppose. Or maybe it was the sun or the Saturday. I went along with it.

"That's General to you, babe."

They all immediately chimed in with a "wooooo."

Must've been the fact it was a Saturday.

"Come on. We're here for a reason," I said, and they all calmed down and began to listen. I recapped the story of Cindy and Biff and of the power struggle they represented. It would be our job to affect a shift of that power from Biff to Cindy. A victory for Cindy would be a victory for all of those on the wrong end of the relationship power struggle. Pow. We were ready to begin our attack.

Chapter Twelve
CINDY

It was, like, totally bizarre. The professor who interrupted my puking outside the Kingfish was Professor McGrew, a communications professor. I knew it. I had her for the intro course when I was a freshman. It was a good course. She seemed neat, too, which is why I followed her over to the Edible Complex for a cup of coffee. Only I didn't actually drink any coffee as it's not the best thing for a stomach after puking so I had some 7-up and she had some coffee and we talked. Well, mostly she talked.

First, she told me to call her Maggie. Weird, huh? Calling a professor by their first name. Anyhow, Maggie—still weird—said she understood my problems with Biff. She said that even from across the room she could tell from my nonverbal communication that I was upset, and she wanted to help. I didn't really understand how she could help. Then she told me about the War Council. Weird name, right? War Council?

"Yes, War Council," she said. "It's a service some of us at the university are providing for students who are having difficulties with their relationships."

"Why 'War Council'?"

"Well, you know the expression 'all's fair in love and war'?"

"Uh huh."

"We happen to feel that expression is particularly appropriate in today's relationships. And since we are a group of people who want to help others involved in the battle that is love, War Council seemed to fit."

"Oh."

"It just seems to me, Cindy, that you have lost the power in your relationship."

Power? She lost me there. What does power have to do with relationships? All I knew was I loved Biff and I had to be with him, even if he is a scum-sucking fuckface. Okay, so I didn't put it that way.

"What does power have to do with it?"

"It has everything to do with it, Cindy. Remember the beginning of your relationship? Remember how badly... what was his name again?"

"Biff."

"Right. Remember how badly Biff wanted to be with you?"

"Yeah, he used to call me all the time and come by the house and want to study and go for walks and sit and talk. Every time his parents went out of town, we would go to his house and spend the weekend together, just the two of us away from his frat friends and the pressures of school. It was like we were this couple, you know, a real couple. Almost like we were married."

It made me sad to think how good things had been, and I'm afraid I started to cry again. Sometimes I'm such a weenie.

"That's okay. I understand how you feel," she said.

She really did seem to understand.

"And how are things now?"

"Way different. He forgets to call. He stands me up. And... and... well, you saw that girl he was attached to tonight."

"Yes, it showed an incredible lack of respect for you."

"Yeah."

"You deserve better than that."

"Yeah."

"You deserve someone who treats you well."

"Yeah."

"You deserve *Biff* treating you well."

"Yeah."

She really did understand.

"That's what I mean about power. You had it, Cindy, but you gave it up. I'd like to help you get that power back."

"You could make it so that Biff acts the way he did in the beginning?"

"We can make it so that Biff begs to get you back."

I liked that. Biff, the scum-sucking fuckface, begging to get me back? Robert Billingsley V begging for me to be his girlfriend again? Maybe even proposing?

"I think maybe I would like to take you up on your offer."

She smiled. "You won't be sorry."

Two days later, I found myself sitting in a room on campus surrounded by professors. It was a Saturday and the way they looked at me and talked about me as if I wasn't there made me feel like a guinea pig. It was kind of funny. I mean, it was my life they were talking about, but in a way, I wasn't really involved. Too weird.

"I think that we can see that Cindy here suffers from a lack of self-esteem. Over the years, she has put up with Biff's growing lack of attention and instead of standing up to him and demanding respect, she has taken the role of doormat. I think we can also see that this has grown into a classic pressured-insecure dysfunction with Cindy in the role of the insecure partner who craves more attention and Biff the pressured partner who craves space."

I wasn't really sure what she was talking about. How was I a doormat? She looked nice, though. She said her name was Kathy, and she worked in psychological services. I felt like maybe she came and spoke at the house once about the services and how they were open to any student and thinking that she looked nice. Real warm. Like someone's mom, you know?

"So," she continued. "Psychologically, our job will be to build Cindy's self-confidence up while tearing down Biff's need for space. In other words, if we lower Biff's self-esteem—especially in terms of his ability to attract women—we will then create in him a need for security, which he knows he will find with Cindy."

"I think I can help with that."

Professor Hard Ass spoke. That one really confused the shit out of me. What was Professor Hard Ass doing here? I didn't think she even liked people. What was she doing in a group that helped relationships? It never occurred to me that Hard Ass—sorry, her real last name was DeVillier and I was supposed to call her Monique—had a life outside the lecture hall. And yet here she was—and in *jeans*.

"This lad… Robert… I'm sorry but I refuse to call anyone Biff," she said.

That was funny. She said it like it was a dirty word. Like "Biff, pooh."

"This Robert was taking my course last semester. Was. He dropped it before finishing so thank god there are no ethical issues involved. But I do believe I just might have the means with which to scramble his brain a bit. You know, a prototypical mind fuck."

Wow! She sweared! She said fuck! Wow! Even if they were speaking as if I wasn't there, I felt like I was experiencing something not many students would ever come close to: professors in jeans, using first names, and swearing!

"And I think I can work with Cindy here."

This super built guy spoke up. Mike was his name. Supposedly he coached the Cal rugby team. I didn't even know they played rugby at Berkeley, but I guess they did.

"I'll get some of the team on it," he said. "Surreptitiously, of course."

Monique cackled. "Surreptitiously? Nice use of syllables, Coach."

"No strain here, Prof."

Oh snap! What was going on here?

"Okay, kids, settle down."

Maggie spoke. Kids. Funny, huh? They were, like, kind of fun people, you know?

"Now Hallie," Maggie continued. "What do you have for us?"

Professor Wilson stood up. She looked cool. I had never had any of her classes. I wasn't a poli sci major, after all, and she taught these advanced seminars. Bunny was poli sci and was always going on and on about how cool Professor Wilson was. Bunny wanted to be, like, the first female president someday and tried to emulate Professor Wilson as much as possible.

Bunny always said that Professor Wilson could have been a real political bigwig if she hadn't married that wimpy film buff guy, Randy. Nobody could figure out what she saw in him.

Even now, he just sat there grinning. Like, what was he thinking?

Hallie stood up and walked to the front of the room—took command of the room, I should say.

"Okay, we've heard Kathy's analysis and know what our objectives are: to beat down Biff's self-esteem while building up Cindy's. Randy and I have worked out the strategy for what we're calling—and Monique already referred to—Operation Mindfuck and feel that the best way to tackle the situation is to hit Biff in his own territory, which is…"

Hallie flipped over the blackboard to reveal a chart on the back. It showed the layout of…

"The Kingfish. Biff's turf. His castle, if you will. From our research, we have learned the man spends more time there than any other bar in town. Our agenda should then revolve around how best to hit him where he lives. His security zone. Timing wise, we have to hit tonight. Not only is it Saturday night—aka date night—but…"

She pulled down another chart. I couldn't figure out what this one was, but it had dates and lines all over it.

"…astrologically, we are in superb position. See how mercury is retrograding over here?"

She pointed to one of the lines, and everyone got this quizzical look like, "no, we have no idea what you are talking about," but she looked secure.

"Mercury, as you may know, is the communication planet. When mercury is in retrograde, all hell breaks loose. Never sign a contract when mercury is in retrograde or expect to understand what your spouse or coworker or really anybody is saying. Perfect timing to fuck with Biff's mind a bit."

There it was again: a swear word. This was getting more and more fun. Fuck with Biff's mind. They knew just what Biff needed.

"So, we hit tonight. Cindy, your job is to make sure that Biff will be at the Kingfish. Can you do that?" Hallie asked.

"You want me to ask him to the Kingfish?"

"No, our plan is to get him there alone."

"Oh, okay. I think I can get his fraternity brother Kevin, Kevin Reynolds, to do it," I said.

"Kevin Reynolds? Senior? Blond hair?" Kathy asked.

"Yeah, you know him?"

"Yes."

She didn't say how, but I supposed he must have come to psychological services. Wow. I wondered why Kevin would go to psychological services—and what he said to Kathy. Interesting. Kathy turned to the others.

"I think he will help."

"Good," Hallie said. "Okay, so, we get Biff to the Kingfish. Let's say 9 o'clock. Once he's there, Monique will go to work. You know what to do?"

"Yes."

"Okay, now, a little while after Monique goes to work—let's say 9:30—does that give you enough time?"

"Plenty."

"You seem pretty self-assured," Mike cracked.

"You've never seen me in action."

"Woooo."

"Okay, you two," Hallie continued. "At about 9:30, Cindy will come through the door with Mike and the rugby guys. Now, Cindy, we have to talk about clothes."

"Clothes?" What was wrong with my clothes?

"Everything is wrong with your clothes."

"Like what?"

"I'm sorry, honey, but button-down shirts and baggy shorts are not sexy. Sorry, Monique, I know how you feel about the objectification of women."

"No offense taken," Monique said. "We're all working toward a common goal here, and sometimes a little packaging helps."

My turn. "Well, I wouldn't wear a button-down shirt and shorts on a Saturday night anyway."

"What would you wear?"

"Maybe a sweater and jeans," I said.

"Yeah, no. Do you have anything maybe a little tighter? A little shorter?"

Not really. Most of my clothes were on the preppy side. That's what everybody wore. Really. Well, everybody in the sorority house. Okay, everybody who was kind of preppy in the sorority house. Mostly the freshmen. Okay, so maybe I hadn't really changed my look since I was a freshman.

"I'll take her shopping this afternoon," said Maggie.

"Great," Hallie continued. "What's important about the evening is that Cindy enter with the guys, appear to be having a fabulous time and then leave. Make sure that Biff notices you. And— this is the most important—do not appear to notice anything Monique does to him."

"Does to him?"

"Monique will be showing Biff a lot of attention, and you have to appear as if you don't care at all, because after you leave, she's going to drop him like a hot potato."

"Absolutely," Monique said.

"Oh." I thought about that for a moment. Part of me was gleeful at the thought of Biff's being all heated up and then dumped. There was a teensy part of me that felt kind of sorry for him, but then I remembered him slobbering all over Kitty and I wasn't sorry anymore.

"Now, do you have a place you can stay tonight after the Kingfish?" Hallie continued.

"Yeah." Bunny was now living in an apartment off campus. I could stay there. She said I was always welcome, and besides, I knew she'd be at Kirk's. She was always at Kirk's.

"Perfect, because Biff may try to contact you after being dumped, and you need to be gone, and you need to turn off your phone completely. This should make him a bit nuts. Actually, the longer you can stay away and avoid looking at your phone, the better. If you could essentially disappear until Monday, that would definitely help our strategy."

"Okay."

"Randy, honey, do you have anything to add?"

"Just that you really need to play your role in this scenario, or it's not going to work, Cindy. You have to appear to be happy as a clam, the belle of the ball, or Biff is going to see through our little script, okay? We're here to help you, but you have to help us help you, okay?"

"Okay."

"Tonight, you might feel like you are being mean to Biff, but just remember that we're working so that you two will ultimately be happier," Randy said.

I was starting to see why Hallie liked Randy so much. Okay, he was kind of wimpy. But he was really sweet, and he really seemed to want to help. They all seemed to want to help and looked over at me expectantly. I wasn't sure what they wanted from me. I mean, if I took them at face value, they just wanted to create happiness for me. It's not that I wasn't grateful; I was. But why? Why me?

I tried to smile and look as self-assured as they did. They all smiled at me, their eyes glistening with expectations: professors with first names, jeans, and swear words trying to help me with my love life.

At that moment, I thought that things had gotten as bizarre as they could get. I was wrong.

Chapter Thirteen
KATHY

I left Brian with the kids and headed across the Bay Bridge toward Berkeley. I was meeting Maggie at, of all places, the Kingfish. I couldn't believe it. I was 34 years old, a married woman with children in grammar school, and I was going to spend my Saturday night at that den of iniquity, the Kingfish. If Berkeley was the dating pool, then the Kingfish was its spawning ground. I don't mean to sound overly dramatic, but the place just reeked of sex—unbridled undergraduate libido-induced sex.

Obviously, it made for the perfect site for the War Council to go to work on Biff. Still, I didn't understand why I had to be there. But Maggie insisted. Although at first hesitant, I then realized I could use the time with Maggie to try and overcome Nick's blunder.

I couldn't believe none of us had thought of it before. None of us had asked Nick how long he was staying in the Bay Area or if he was planning to do any time abroad—a natural question to ask of a French literature student. I knew that Maggie could not take being left again, and yet somehow it never occurred to me to make sure that Nick wasn't going anywhere—or that he would be stupid it enough to bring it up if he was.

We would have to make sure we were more thorough in our future questioning. Not that I was ready to accept the War Council as an alternative to individual growth or counseling. I wasn't. Still, if we were going to use the methods, we should have done it right. Been more thorough. If Maggie had been in on it, she would have thought of it, with her ability to address every angle. But she wasn't in on the AWAC, she was its target, so we didn't have the use of her brain. We had to go it alone, which meant I had to go it alone with Maggie in a booth at the Kingfish.

The place was a greasy cesspool. I saw that Maggie had staked out the most strategic spot in the place—a booth with a complete view of the pub. From her vantage point, she could see the bar area, the table area, and the path from the front door to the bathrooms. No one could enter or exit without being spotted. She could also overhear most of the conversations at the bar. I walked over and took my seat across from her.

Maggie leaned over and whispered furtively, "Quick, order a beer."

"Why?"

"Because we have to look like we belong."

"We don't belong, Maggie. This is a bar for college students and those yearning to relive their college days."

"Well, then yearn a little."

"Oh, Maggie."

"Kathy, stop the psychoanalysis and have a little fun. Forget you're a fuddy duddy. Oh, and before I forget, after..."

I didn't let her finish. "Me? A fuddy duddy?"

"Yeah, it's a Saturday night. We're out at the hottest bar in Berkeley, well, Oakland. Berkeley adjacent. Whatever. Let go and have some fun."

"It seems to me it should be you who lets go."

"Me?" She looked at me warily.

"Yeah, you." I let her stew a minute before I let her have it. "How's Nick?"

"I was wondering how long it would take you to bring him up."

"Well?"

"There's nothing to say."

"I think there's a lot to say."

"What?"

"Come on, Maggie. What happened?"

"Nothing. That's just it. Nothing happened." She tried to smile as if nothing was wrong but that wasn't true.

"Why? What happened to 'let go and have fun'?"

"I can't do it, Kathy. I can't start something knowing it can't go anywhere. If I didn't like him so much, it would be okay. I could just have a fling. But with Nick, I just can't."

140

Her turmoil made me realize that Maggie had fallen for Nick. Part of me was ecstatic. Please, God, let her finally be over Bill. But part of me also felt the pain she felt. The terror at giving into her feelings again. Funny how that is with friends. You go through the ups and downs so often that you feel what they feel. For all our differences and misunderstandings, Maggie and I had always been there for each other.

The part of me that could feel her pain questioned my actions in helping her fall for a man who could potentially hurt her, but I didn't see that hiding from love had helped. Maybe learning to love Nick whether or not he was leaving was the answer. Maybe it was the key to helping her get over Bill. I hoped so. I had to hope so.

"Maggie, no one knows what the future will bring. How can you stop from enjoying yourself now for something that may or may not happen? I mean, come on. Nick might not go to Paris, or he might ask you to go with him, or you might realize he's not right for you."

Maggie looked around the Kingfish to see what was happening, and I knew I had to pull out the big guns.

"Okay, well, what if Bill returns? What would happen to Nick then? What would you do? Do you know?"

Maggie looked at me, surprised. Aha. She hadn't thought of that this time. She really had been letting go of Bill. Slowly, but it was happening.

"You don't know, do you, Maggie? The fact is you don't know if he will ever return, just as Nick doesn't know if he will go to Paris. Why spoil a beautiful present with a great guy because of an uncertain future?"

I could see I was beginning to get to her, but just then the floor show began.

Biff entered.

It was almost nine. Right on schedule. Kevin Reynolds came in behind him. Kevin nodded in our direction but otherwise showed no recognition. I smiled. It was such a coincidence that I knew Kevin, although not so unusual, I suppose. Although Berkeley is a large institution, the Greek system is a relatively small social system, and Cindy and Biff were integral members of that system, so perhaps it wasn't too unusual that I would have had one of their friends as a client. It was Kevin's personality that was unusual.

Kevin was a very sweet boy, just charming. He had been coming into SPS sporadically the past two years—about the time he began suffering from an identity crisis. Kevin had joined the fraternity as a freshman, and at the time, was very much into being one of the "bros." Coming from a small town in Idaho, it gave him a social life, friends, and an identity.

During his junior year, though, Kevin suddenly wasn't sure he fit that identity and really not sure he wanted to fit the identity. He started seeing the fraternity—the whole Greek system, really—in a different light. You might say he had a revelation, but it was triggered by a sociology class taught by one of Monique's colleagues.

Professor Camille Kent was famous for her class on social stereotyping. Active in human rights issues, Camille was a charismatic lecturer who inspired many a student to become more involved. Kevin ate the course up. He was one of those students who really became immersed in his classes and loved learning—like I said, just charming.

Through Kevin I knew Biff, or at least I knew stories about people like Biff. Maggie was ecstatic. I told her I could not reveal anything that Kevin had told me, but I could help with a personality profile on a prototypical member of their fraternity and the fraternity mentality. Because Kevin was questioning the fraternity, he spilled his guts on everything that went on in the house. It was an eye-opening experience to say the least and included everything from the macabre (stealing cadavers from the medical school) to the barbaric (throwing an empty keg at a potential love interest).

And now Kevin stood at the Kingfish with someone I assumed to be one of the worst offenders. Now, I never knew if Biff stole cadavers or tossed a beer keg, but from what we had gathered from Cindy, the potential was definitely there. I examined Biff's face to see what I could gather. He was handsome enough but had snotty old-money WASP superiority plastered all over his face. It had the effect of making him appear cold, the type that might become less good looking the more you got to know him.

"Do you think he's good looking?" Maggie nodded toward Biff.

"Maybe superficially, but there doesn't seem to be anything to back it up. No substance," I said.

"Uh huh. Do you, uh, think Nick is good looking?"

Aha! My little speech had gotten her to think.

"Are you kidding? Nick is very handsome."

"But not better looking than Bill."

"Uh, yeah, much better looking than Bill."

I couldn't believe Maggie thought Bill was better looking than Nick. I guess that's what love—and time—does to a person. Bill was nice looking, but Nick was much more traditionally handsome.

"Really?"

"Really."

We pondered that over our beers for a second. Then Monique entered. It was nine o'clock sharp. Now, I've gotta tell you, Monique is a woman who knows how to make an entrance. She had on a short black leather skirt, a white camisole top, and a tuxedo jacket draped over her shoulders. Monique's got these really long legs that were only accentuated by the black tights that traveled down to black heels. She stood in the doorway for a moment as every head turned to look at her. I could tell she was reveling just a bit in the effect it was having. She enjoyed freaking the college crowd out a bit every now and then with her image.

Monique made a point of checking out the scene before sauntering over and taking a seat next to Biff at the bar. The boy looked like he might faint on the spot.

"Well, hello, Robert."

"Uh, hi, Professor DeVillier."

"Call me Monique. We're off campus and you're not taking my class anymore."

"Yeah, about that…"

"Shhh. Like I said, we're off campus now." She took a look around. "So, this is where you students congregate."

"Yeah, the Kingfish is the place to be."

"I thought so," she said. "Actually, I was hoping I just might find you here."

"Me?" His voice actually squeaked.

"Oh, Robert, don't you know how fascinating I find you?"

Monique looked deep into his eyes. At first, I thought Biff might slide off his barstool, but soon his bluster took over and the cocky spirit returned. This would be his undoing.

"I've been told I have that effect on women."

What a bozo, right? Maggie and I snickered. Even Kevin rolled his eyes and left to sit with some friends. I know Monique was probably having a hard time keeping a straight face, but she kept up her role. She moved maybe an inch closer to him, which had a perceptible physical reaction on poor Biff. We were banking on the ole teacher-student seduction fantasy—a very popular fantasy among males in Biff's age group, I have to say.

"If you would like, Robert, you may buy me a drink."

"Well, sure, Prof, uh, Mon, uh, sure."

A flash of the little boy came back, and he still couldn't bring himself to use her first name. That was a good sign. Now we just had to wait for Cindy to arrive and the fireworks would really begin.

Monique had already caused Biff to have to rush off to the men's room three times by the time Cindy arrived. Luckily, he was back at the bar and putting his embarrassingly bad moves on Monique when Cindy entered.

It was another grand entrance. Cindy looked absolutely enchanting. She was wearing a very pretty cotton print sundress that was, at once, very feminine and figure flattering. Maggie had astutely helped Cindy find an outfit that would not compete with the kind of ensemble Monique was wearing. Cindy had pulled her hair back to show off her pretty face and was accompanied by a hulking god of a man.

"Who is that?" I asked Maggie.

"One of Mike's rugby players. Connor. He's Australian."

"He's unbelievable."

"Yeah, Mike did good. Listen, do you think that Nick was upset about what happened last night?"

I snapped my head back from the Adonis to concentrate on Maggie.

"Of course, he is. He really likes you, Maggie. In fact, I'm sure he's sitting home tonight wondering if he's going to hear from you."

Okay, so I knew he was home waiting to hear from her.

"Maybe you should go over and at least talk to him, Maggie. Let him know how you feel…"

"Maybe."

Cindy moved through the crowd with Connor, and they took their place about five barstools away from Biff and Monique. I noticed Kevin looking over at Cindy with a stunned look and wondered if there was anything between them— it wasn't something he'd discussed with me.

Biff looked over at Cindy and seemed rather surprised that she was there with such a hunk, but when Monique threatened to move away (I think she got about a quarter of an inch), Biff turned his attention back to her.

"Who is that?" Monique inquired of Biff.

"No one important."

His smarmy smile sickened me. What a prick. Luckily, Cindy continued to play her part and giggled and flirted with Connor at the bar. He seemed to be making it easy for her. Just as I wondered where Mike was, he slid into the booth.

"Howdydoo, ladies. What's up?"

The guy definitely had energy. Mike was a real character—a big lovable bear of a guy once you got past the macho posturing.

"How's my boy doing?"

Mike looked over at Connor and Cindy, who were toasting their drinks and grinning.

"I've got backups ready to go in at a moment's notice, should we need them." Then Mike noticed Monique with Biff. "Woah, baby. Is that Hard Ass? Nice. Very nice. Say, when's the server coming by? Are there servers, or do I have to go to the bar?"

"It's easier if you go to the bar."

"Gotcha. I'll go give Hard Ass a little ogle and be right back. Before I do, should I send another guy in to hit on Cindy? No, I'll wait. No, maybe I won't. Okay, see ya."

With that, Mike took off, winked at Monique, sidled up to another husky guy, and ordered a drink. The husky guy then made a point of passing directly in front of Biff and Monique to yell, "Hey, Cindy—haven't seen you since the party at Phil's."

The husky guy then sidled up to Cindy, gave her a big hug and a kiss on the cheek, and began chatting away. Cindy looked surprised but went along with it. Biff again noticed and showed perhaps a twinge of being bothered, but then Monique recrossed her legs, and he quickly returned his attention to her.

Maggie turned back from watching the group at the bar. "Is it me or does this place just reek of sex?"

"Thinking of Nick?"

"No, no, well, yeah. I guess I'm just confused."

"Don't you think he is, too?"

"What do you mean?"

"Maggie, if I've learned anything from counseling people, it's that we are all scared shitless, especially of being vulnerable. But life is too short and too precious to hide ourselves in a closet because we're scared. We have to act on our feelings. Yes, we might get hurt, but at least we feel. Come on, Maggie, don't you know how rare it is to find someone you care about the way you care about Nick?"

"Yeah, I do. Want to know what's really funny about Nick?"

"What?"

"He seems to understand me so well—practically anticipates my every move."

"That's great." Okay, so the anticipating thing was the AWAC, and I felt a small tinge of guilt but, hey, it was making her feel good.

"Okay, yeah, okay." Maggie pulled out her phone and walked outside to get some quiet.

Whoosh—all this drama was exhausting. I turned back to look at the scene at the bar. It was playing out nicely. Monique and Biff had their heads burrowed close. Cindy now had four guys around her and seemed to be enjoying herself. The next thing I knew Kevin had taken Maggie's place in the booth.

"Hi, Dr. Fischer."

"Kevin. Thank you for coming and helping out."

"With the way Biff treats Cindy, I'm happy to help—only, who are the guys?"

"Friends, why?"

"Oh, nothing."

"Kevin, do you have feelings for Cindy?"

Kevin took a deep breath. He'd had a few drinks, and they were taking their toll. The boy had definitely not developed a tolerance for alcohol in the fraternity. He looked up, his blue eyes peeking out from under his curly blond bangs.

"I am hopelessly in love with her."

It was so sweet I didn't know whether to laugh or cry.

"Why don't you tell her?"

"Are you kidding? She is so blinded by Mr. Biff, the fifth, she doesn't know I exist, except as a friend."

He said it with such anguish. Ah, young love, young seemingly unrequited love. I remembered how cute Brian was when he first admitted he loved me. He was 19, and it troubled him so completely. Love. The great equalizer. It makes us all so vulnerable, and when it hits—really hits—for the first time, we just can't figure out what the hell is happening.

I wondered what Cindy did feel for Kevin. Maybe she just didn't know, but unfortunately, before I could press Kevin any further, Maggie returned.

"He said to come over," she said. "What do I do now?"

Then she spotted Kevin. "Oh, hey. Kevin, right? Thanks for the help."

"It was nothing. Gotta go."

Kevin vaulted from the booth. "Thanks, Dr. Fischer."

"Come see me next week, Kevin. Anytime."

"Yeah, okay."

The poor lovesick boy slid through the crowd and out the door. Having revealed his feelings, he now needed escape. I noticed Cindy noticing him leave. Hmmm… I had to cut short my musing and return to Maggie who was now a bundle of nerves.

"So, Maggie, he wants to talk?"

"Yeah, said to come over anytime. What do I do?"

"Go. I'll finish up here."

"You will?"

"Yes, I will make sure it all goes according to plan. Go. You'll feel better."

"I will?"

"Yes, you will."

"Maybe I should wait."

"Go now, while it's on your mind."

"It would be good to talk, to explain…"

"Of course it would."

"Okay, I'm going." But she didn't move.

"Okay, here I go. Do I look okay?"

"You look great. Now get out of here."

"Okay."

She nodded a couple times and finally left the booth. Yeesh. Does love make us weenies or what? Maggie left and soon I was joined by Mike.

"Where's the Gen off to?"

"She has something to take care of."

"Left you at the helm, eh?"

"If you want to call it that."

"Time for the finale, right?"

"Right."

"Gotcha. See you back at the offices."

Mike jumped up from the table before I had a chance to ask him what he meant by that. We weren't meeting back at the offices tonight— unless Maggie forgot to tell me in her Nick-addled state. Oh well, Mike would figure it out when no one showed up.

Mike went up to the growing bevy of dudes surrounding Cindy and said, very loudly (so Biff could hear), "Hey guys, let's continue this party elsewhere."

"All right."

"Cool, coach."

Mike, Cindy, and the guys all trooped out together. Once outside, they would disperse. That was the plan, anyway. Maybe Cindy and the Adonis she came in with had hit it off. Hard to say. In any event, the illusion would then end. I must admit that Mike's group did a helluva job playing their parts. I wondered how he had gotten them to participate—he must be a really good coach.

Biff noticed the noisy departure of Cindy and the guys but quickly returned to his attempted seduction of Monique.

"So, Monique..."

Aha, he had come around to using her first name.

"…would you, you know, like to get out of here and head up to my place?"

Monique looked at Biff for a moment. A long moment.

Then she burst out laughing, a wild raucous laugh that quieted the entire bar. Monique then said, loud enough for everyone—even those in the toilets, I'm guessing—to hear:

"What a yutz! Did you really expect me to leave with *you*?"

Everyone started laughing. There were some cat calls, and Biff began to turn scarlet.

"As if you could seduce me. You poor boy. The truth is, I don't think you're up to it."

The crowd went "oooh."

"Let's face it, you couldn't even handle my *class*."

The crowd went "aaah."

Monique patted his red cheeks. "But you can dream."

And with that, Monique made her exit, and the entire bar began to clap. Okay, so I started it. But the other patrons—many of whom seemed to know him—soon joined in. I wondered how popular Biff really was.

At first, Biff looked like he wanted to crawl under the bar but instead plastered his snottiest, hardest look onto his face and turned to the bar. A drunk collegiate came up to him.

"Trying to seduce a prof, Biff? Pretty tricky stuff."

"Fuck off."

With that, Biff swaggered out the door and the drunk made a face to his friends, who all went "woooo."

With all of the mini-dramas tied up, I figured it was time to head home. I looked at my watch. It was 10:30. The whole thing had taken a little over two hours. Incredible. I was exhausted. All this love and sex and drama was incredibly tiresome—and yet somehow exhilarating. In a way, Maggie was right. This dating stuff was a battlefield—one in which the battle itself was exhausting but the victories exhilarating.

As I drove home, I began to look forward to crawling into bed with Brian. I hoped he wasn't asleep so I could tell him everything that happened. I thought about all that had transpired that night and realized how lucky I was to have found my soulmate so early in life.

As I crossed the Bay Bridge, I remembered Mike's comment about meeting back at the War Council offices. Had Maggie asked Mike and Monique to meet her back there? She left without saying a word to me about it. Oh well, I was too tired to think about going back. Besides, Mike and Monique could figure things out on their own.

Chapter Fourteen
MONIQUE

I want to make one thing perfectly clear: I did not make the first move. I just didn't. I'll admit I was feeling rather randy that night. You can't spend two hours in the Kingfish and not feel randy. And I must admit I was looking for an outlet for all that pent-up sexuality. An outlet was all. But I did not make the first move.

Maggie had asked me to meet her back at the War Council office after the encounter at the Kingfish—kind of a post-mortem for the evening. Frankly, my part went incredibly well. The boy was incredibly easy to manipulate—any boy with an ego that substantial is easy prey. And because I couldn't really see what else was going on, I was eager to swap stories with Maggie, Kathy, and, okay, Mike.

I reached the War Council offices and found Mike. I had to admit he was looking rather good in the afterglow of our adventures at the Kingfish. He was sitting in the back corner in a

partitioned-off space that Maggie had deco-
rated to look warmer than the main room as it
would serve as the interview area for potential
clients. Maggie thought it should have a modicum of privacy and a warm touch, almost like a
therapist's office. Mike was sitting on the couch,
so I took a seat in the chair next to the couch.

"Where are Maggie and Kathy?" I asked.

"Dunno."

"Now there's a scintillating response."

Silence. That was strange. Not only did Mike
not respond to my barb, he had refrained from
calling me Hard Ass or cookie or babycakes.
And he was looking at me rather quizzically.

"What?" I asked.

"You really put the moves on that boy tonight."

I shrugged. "That was my job."

"I was impressed," he said.

"Oh, you were?" Now I looked quizzically at
him. What was this all about?

"Yeah, I was."

"Should I be flattered?"

"Whatever. I'm just stating a fact."

"Oh, a fact."

"Yeah, a fact."

"Well, from what I could see, you were holding
your own."

"I guess. Mostly it was my boys. I was just the
master manipulator."

"The master manipulator?" Somehow, I found
that hysterically funny, and I started to laugh. I
don't know why, but I was feeling rather giddy.

I guess it gave me a high to get that Robert so worked up—kind of a power trip.

"What's so funny?" he asked.

"I don't know, Master Manipulator. I guess I just have this image of you flying around in a mask and cape propelling unsuspecting rugby players into the Kingfish mating pool. 'Here he comes, boy and girls, the master manipulator: No dating couple is safe as long as he is patrolling the bars and pubs.'"

"Well, no man is safe if you are in the room."

That floored me. "Oh, really?"

"Yeah, really."

"So… you don't feel safe?"

"I do not."

"You feel that you are in danger?"

"Imminent danger."

Imminent? For a split second, I thought about making a crack but decided to refrain. "What do you think might happen?"

"Anything can happen."

"Anything?"

We locked eyes. I just couldn't believe how sexually attracted I was to this creature sitting next to me. But, dammit, I was. I mean, he was cute. He was built. He hadn't belched or farted or performed any other obnoxious acts in the last five minutes. I was definitely craving some action, and he seemed to be craving some action, and Kathy and Maggie were nowhere to be seen.

A million thoughts raced through my head. Should we go call Maggie and Kathy? Should we go? Should we talk? But we didn't say a word. We just sat there with our eyes locked with just the sound of our breathing—and it was not light breathing—in the room. The electrical current running between us threatened to blow a fuse.

And then suddenly we were kissing. It was passionate bordering on the animalistic. In short, it was great. The fact that Maggie or Kathy could walk in on us at any moment—although it was pretty obvious at that point that they weren't coming—made it all the more passionate and illicit and dangerous. Oh so dangerous.

Mike was a great kisser. A great kisser. I put my arms around his neck and pulled closer. He had a strong body, and I could feel it tingle as I pressed against it. Then I noticed his arms had goosebump. How cute is that? He was nervous. I pulled back and looked into his eyes and saw a flicker of a little boy afraid of being hurt. That shocked me. His image was so crude, so insensitive—always spouting all that shit about being a real man—but in his eyes I saw something else. He was a big ole marshmallow. Suddenly, I saw the Mike he hid from the world, and it made him *so* much more attractive.

My kisses took on a more urgent quality. I wanted to assure him it was okay and envelop him with my body. We fell onto the couch, still fully clothed, and after some heavy petting, he seemed to be attempting speech.

"Oh god."

"I know, feels great."

"Fuck great. It feels fanfuckingtastic."

"That's the word: fanfuckingtastic."

"I love this. I mean, you know, this connection."

"It's great."

"Fuck great," we both said at the same time and then laughed, continued kissing, and started peeling each other's clothes off (not an easy task when you are lying on a couch).

"Okay, okay, I've got this…"

"No, don't put that there, my arm will get stuck…"

"Oh, okay. Ow!"

"Sorry."

"That's okay. It's just… the zipper."

"Yeow."

We both laughed wildly and ended up rolling onto the floor, leaving the clothes behind. Luckily, the carpet was a soft ply the university had just put in. In this instance, I decided that the university really knew where to put their money.

"This is great." I must admit I was genuinely shocked at how great it was.

"Great?"

"Great."

"Fantastic?"

"Fantastic. Really fantastic. You're fantastic."

"No, you're fantastic."

"Ha—do we sound like lovesick cows or what?"

We both laughed.

"I know. Luckily, we both know this is just physical," Mike said, and I was so relieved he saw what we were doing for what it was.

"Totally. It's fantastic—no, phenomenal—and yet, just physical. Who could ask for more?"

"Not me. And, of course, we can keep doing this if we want."

"Sure we can, because we know we won't get involved."

"Right, and we don't have to worry about the future."

"Exactly, because we know it's just physical. Phenomenally physical."

"Yeah." Mike began kissing me more urgently. "Oh so phenomenally physical."

And then he—how should I say this delicately—climaxed, and in a bit of a unique twist, yelled out "Go Cal" with an intensity that had me both laughing hysterically and worried that the campus security might come bursting through the door to find us lying naked on the brand new university carpet.

Mike looked at me, still smiling, and took me into his arms. "What?" he asked.

"Us."

"Yeah, I know."

"Did you ever in a million...?"

"Never."

"Me, either."

"But it was good."

"That it was."

I smiled at him. That it was.

"You know, if we keep this up, we'll probably burn out," he said.

"Definitely. It's just physical. We'll definitely burn out."

"As great as it is… and it is great."

"It is great." He got this devilish look in his eyes.

"What?"

"Nothing."

"What?"

"Nothing. Just thinking about doing some exploring…"

"Exploring?"

"Yup." He grinned and began kissing me again and, well, let's just say that although I didn't yell out "Go Cal," I certainly understood the sentiment.

Chapter Fifteen
NICK

Music. Its importance in a relationship cannot be underestimated. Let me rephrase that. It's importance in creating a mood for a relationship cannot be underestimated–at least for me–and tonight, especially, the mood had to be just right. Just right. Maggie was coming any minute, and I needed the mood to be just right.

I was flipping through my digital library. Piaf was playing, but I could sense it wasn't right for what I was going for. Besides, I was beginning to feel that Piaf had betrayed me. She was singing *"je ne regrette rien"*–I regret nothing–and here I was regretting just about everything.

I regretted being so cavalier about how I had treated Maggie. I regretted telling her about Paris. I regretted that I was relying on others so much in our relationship. I regretted that I regretted so much and that these stupid obsessive voices were spinning in my head. Most of all, I regretted having to sit here in my apartment listening to

Edith Piaf's self-righteousness pouring out of the speakers. Shut up, Edith.

I flipped over to Milton Nascimiento. Light Brazilian jazz. Maybe the mood from the night at the Rio Dio would spill into the room. No, that wasn't right either. I had a flash of her eyes burning brightly as we danced, then another flash of them being extinguished by my words. The hurt. I remembered the hurt reflected in her eyes. This music brought up memories of that vision. Shut up, Milton.

I went back to perusing my collection. I have a pretty substantial collection of music. Each of my studies had brought my attention to a different genre of music, and I loved and downloaded them all.

I realized I hadn't looked at anything in the classical library from my music history days at Indiana University. Classical music can be incredibly romantic—and soothing. That's what I needed. A little romance to show Maggie I cared, and a little soothing to quench her fears.

But what classical? Hmmmm. I felt like Ravel and Rachmaninov were a bit overdone in the romance department. Too obvious. I didn't want obvious. I wanted lyrical. I wanted… Chopin. I put on a collection of his piano works. Yes. Lightness. Grace. This would be perfect.

Okay, what else? I don't know. What do you mean what else? What else should I do to prepare for Maggie's arrival is what else! Maggie's arrival. She wasn't even here yet, and the obsessive questions swirled about in my brain like vultures circling their unsuspecting prey. I didn't like that. I didn't like to feel that I was prey or that I was unsuspecting. I am not. I am a man, dammit. I am in control of my life and my feelings.

I mean, who is this woman that she makes me feel like this? Okay, so she's beautiful and intelligent. She's got wacky ideas about love—that's what she's got. And she's rather possessive, don't you think? So what if I'm going to Paris next year? Why can't we enjoy what we have now? If she is too sensitive to let go and enjoy what we have, then maybe we shouldn't get involved. Before I gave into the impulse to flip back over to Edith and exclaim to the world *"je ne regrette rien,"* there was a knock at the door.

She was here. Maggie was here. I looked around to see if everything looked all right. I suppose it looked all right. What if it didn't look all right? What would she do? Would she leave without another glance and think that I am a slob or a grown man who can't keep a decent apartment? What are you thinking? You really think a woman is going to leave because of the way your apartment—a temporary university apartment, I might add—looks? Stop obsessing and answer the door, you nimnal. Oh, please God, let this evening go well.

"Hello."

She looked radiant. She reeked of beer and grease from the Kingfish and yet still looked radiant.

"Hi."

We stood there on the doorstep for a moment while I lost myself in her gaze. Soon, I snapped out of it. "Come in. How are you?"

"I'm okay. You?"

"Okay."

Now we stood in the hallway. Awkward! "Shall we sit down?"

"Oh." I snapped out of it again. "Of course. Come in. Sit down."

We sat down on the infamous couch from the night before. The dangerous scary couch that she had fled from in terror. Would the couch have the same effect tonight? Did she notice it was the same couch? SNAP OUT OF IT, BOY.

"Would you like something to drink?"

"Yes."

"Okay. What?"

"Whatever."

"Okay."

Whatever. What the hell did that mean? I had a bottle of pinot noir that I'd opened. Pinot's romantic, don't you think?

"How about a glass of pinot?"

She smiled at me. Yes. Good choice, man. She took the glass and sipped from it. I sat down beside her, and a horrible wrenching moment of silence pervaded the room.

"Pretty music. It's very… soothing."

Yes! She smiled at me. Good choice, man. "It's Chopin."

"Oh."

The horrible wrenching silence again fell upon us. I was so afraid I'd say something stupid or something that would send her fleeing again that I said nothing. Nothing was about as awful as something stupid, but truthfully I couldn't think of anything to say, period.

"Listen, Nick…"

"Yes?"

"I want to apologize for last night."

"No need to apologize."

"I shouldn't have left without telling you why," she said. "I'm just so scared of being hurt again. I know that sounds stupid—I'm 30 years old and still afraid of being hurt. Stupid, huh?"

"Nothing you could do would be stupid."

"See, that's just the problem. You are so sweet to me. I'm just not used to this."

"To what?"

"To being loved."

Maggie looked up at me and gave a weak smile. Oh, how I adored this woman.

"I do love you, Maggie. I know it sounds crazy. We haven't known each other for very long, and we don't know what will happen, but I want you to know that. And don't think I say those words lightly because I don't. No matter what happens, it will not change how I feel about you. If you walk out right now, I will go on loving you. That's what feelings are, Maggie. They stay with us.

They don't die. The love you had for Bill hasn't died. It shouldn't. But it also shouldn't stop you from letting me in."

I paused a moment to brush a tear off her cheek.

"…and if I go to Paris, maybe we can…"

"No." Maggie put a finger to my mouth to stop me. "Let's not worry about the future. Let's just enjoy what we have now, here, together."

And then she kissed me. None of the women I had been with before prepared me for how I felt about this woman who was pressing her lips to mine. We moved to the bedroom, and with Chopin as our background music, were finally able to express all those feelings.

Everything that had gone before this moment came crashing through my mind: my first glimpse of Maggie at the dinner party, the specks of gold in her green eyes, the meetings at Café Strada, *Sabrina*, the walks on campus, the Kingfish, dancing at the Rio Dio, holding hands on the beach, the first kiss, the couch…

Later, as she slept, I held her in my arms and stared at her face. She looked so peaceful. I was overjoyed to finally see her like that. We slept the rest of the night lying in each other's arms and enjoying the bond that had been created—a bond that I prayed would never be severed.

Chapter Sixteen
KATHY

Needless to say, the War Council was an unqualified success. We were inundated with business after word began to spread around campus about the Kingfish incident and all that followed. As I sat at Café Strada, I mused on our success and what it said about the current state of love in our society.

It was summer. The summers at Berkeley were very special to me. Not as many students so my workload was less, and I felt I had the campus to myself. Even Café Strada was less crowded, I noticed, as I sat waiting for Maggie to join me for our weekly latte. The place was still relatively full, just not the packed throngs that crowded it during the school year. And there were still any number of mini-dramas being played out around me as I sat sipping my latte.

Poor lost souls. Just look at them. So scared of each other. Scared to feel—to love.

"Hi, Dr. Fischer."

I was so intent on the actions of the people milling about the café that I didn't notice Kevin Reynolds walk up to my table. He looked miserable, his blue eyes peering out from behind his blond bangs and giving him more than ever the look of a sheepdog puppy.

"Kevin, how are you?"

"Okay. Interviewing in the city."

"Post-graduation blues?"

"Life blues."

I laughed. "Life blues? That's heavy."

He didn't see the humor. "Yeah, you graduate, and everything feels great for about two weeks. And then it hits you: You've finished 22 years of your life and have no idea who you are or where you're going. All those years I had an identity: I was a student. And then suddenly I'm not. I guess I just don't know who I am anymore."

Ah, the drama of youth. "Whatever it is you decide to be, Kevin, I'm sure you will do just fine."

"Yeah, some start. Unemployed, unloved, uninspired. Oh well, see ya, Dr. Fischer."

"Okay. Come see me anytime. Just because you've graduated doesn't mean I don't care."

He smiled a weak smile. "Thanks." And then he shuffled off to sit in a corner of the café.

Poor sweet Kevin. He still hadn't told Cindy how he felt.

"Doc! Doc! I'm so glad I caught you."

Before I could ponder more, Betsy, one of our more recent clients walked over. Betsy worked as an administrative assistant for the chair of the biology department and had heard about our services through one of the students. Unlike our typical clients, Betsy was middle-aged and had been married for 30 years. She hired us to help her husband, Herb, become less of a couch potato and pay her more attention.

"Doc, I just wanted to say thanks a heap for all you did for ole Herb and me."

"You are most welcome."

"It's a miracle. That's all I can say—it's a miracle," she said. "Herb has been my Mr. Romeo like never before. That is one super service you kids are running over there, worth every bit the $500 I paid. Worth every bit. I just can't tell you how grand things are, just grand. Well, gotta run. Herb and I are, well, we're having an afternoon rendezvous—so romantic, am I right?"

With that, Betsy bustled off with the glow of a smitten teenager and joined the balding, paunchy man sitting a few tables away.

Love. The great equalizer. I realized that it's not that we are just discovering the trauma of love. The world has always worried about love, dissected it, tried to understand it. Let's face it: Most of the great art from the beginning of time has come from trying to figure out this wondrous, mysterious, torturous emotion that decries logic at every turn.

What we have lost is the sense of community to support us through this wondrous, mysterious, torturous emotion. In many places, the extended family has disappeared, and instead we are left with a group of people more comfortable with their smart phones than with another human being. But our smart phones don't support us through the trauma of love; they do not give us love. There is no mechanism better than another human being to comfort us or to help us through the precarious game of love.

Really, it's not that the world has forgotten how to love; it's that we have been forced to tackle love on our own—a scary proposition that offers no solace if things don't work out. That's why people are afraid to leave relationships that aren't working, to test relationships that are tired, or begin a relationship that isn't, in their minds, perfect—which is impossible due to the nature of human beings. We aren't perfect people.

If we are given a little emotional support through this precarious journey that is love, however, it is not so tragic if we lose that love. No longer are we left with an empty feeling of worthlessness if it doesn't work out. We still have our support system and are therefore less afraid to take a chance.

In other words: We're not scared of love; we're scared of not having love, of not being loved, of being hurt, of being alone. That is, until now.

I could help these people. Well, I mean, the War Council could help these people. I realized I was changing my tune a bit but not really. I was adapting my ideas to the ones represented by

Maggie's original War Council concept. I also had to acknowledge all that we had accomplished.

I still didn't like the name. War Council promoted love as a battle. I preferred to think of us at the U.N. Security Council of love and had tried to get everyone to start just calling us The Council. We promoted peaceful coexistence, not war. Let's bring people together, not send them out battling each other. Naturally, there are times when bringing about a peaceful settlement requires strategies and battle plans, but I liked to think of our strategies and battle plans as more akin to economic sanctions or strategic diplomacy than all-out war.

Take Betsy and Herb: Herb was pretty much spending all his time sitting in his Barcalounger watching television and ignoring Betsy. She nagged Herb to get out of his chair and do something. Herb got irritated and more entrenched in his chair.

So, we worked to reframe the paradigm a bit by creating Betsy as a pleasurable alternative to the television while the same time destroying Herb's desire to watch television. The latter was accomplished in part through negative sense stimuli. Essentially, every time Herb sat down to watch television, he received a small shock from his chair (barely perceptible and not dangerous, I can assure you), a smell sensor set off some rather putrid odors, and the TV set was perpetually out of focus—no matter how many times he called the cable company.

We then helped Betsy realize that the better she felt about herself and the things she did apart from her life with Herb, the more attracted Herb would be to spending time with her. Betsy joined a book club, began working in their garden, going to films with friends, and attending lectures on campus. Suddenly, Herb was bored, lonely, the television wasn't solving his problems, and there was the same vibrant, self-assured woman he'd fallen in love with 30 years ago standing before him.

So, through strategically designed plans, we helped bring happiness to a troubled couple. The War Council—sorry, just Council—provided loving support toward the goal of a peaceful loving union. Really, we were just what the world needed. I had to give Maggie credit for the idea, and the truth is, she was one of its biggest successes. Now that she had lost interest in the project—once she and Nick got together, she slowly started backing away from the project—I could really move it toward its full potential.

"Sorry I'm late. What's up?" Speak of the devil. Maggie slid into the seat across from me.

"Not much. Just enjoying the day."

"It is a nice day, huh?"

"Very nice. Did you see Betsy and Herb over there?"

"Which ones are they?"

"The Bio admin and the couch potato."

"Oh yeah, that was a good one. Did you take the electrodes out of his chair?"

"Randy took care of it."

"Good. Things going all right over at the War Council? I'm going to get over to the offices soon. I promise."

"No worries. Things are moving very smoothly. Mike and Monique have even hired some new field workers to help out."

"Oh good. Good."

"So?"

"So?" Maggie knew what I mean and began grinning from ear to ear.

"How's Nick?"

"Good. Yeah. Good." More grinning. And some blushing, too.

"So?"

"What? Things are good. They're really... good."

"Uh huh?" Details, Maggie, details.

"Actually, things are fantastic. That's why I haven't been around. It's kind of embarrassing, but things are just so good."

"Uh huh?"

"You know what I mean." The smile got bigger. "We've had this project where we're, you know, working our way through his music collection."

"Working your way through?"

"Yeah, you know, from Elvis to Puccini. It's a HUGE project."

Maggie laughed out loud, and I must say my heart was filled with joy. It felt so good to see her happy after all the years of Bill-induced misery. The change was incredible. Two short months and logical, analytical Maggie was grinning like a schoolgirl. Like I said, love: the great equalizer.

"We've even worked our way up to the blues."

"You and Nick are listening to the blues? Together?" That was a big step.

"Well, not just listening, you know..."

Just then the boy wonder showed up.

"Hey gals, what's up?"

"Ha, Nick, that's what I said when I got here, too!" Maggie said.

"You did? Wow!"

He sat down and they looked at each other like two lovesick cows. Does love make us weenies or what?

"Guess what I've been doing, Maggie?"

Needless to say, they were oblivious to me.

"Downloading some new music?"

"Yep." Nick held up his phone to show a photo of an album by Trombone Shorty. "What do you think?"

I swear the woman swooned right on the spot. Then he swooned and their cheeks blushed. It was sickening. "Ahem."

"Oh, Kathy, I'm sorry, um..."

"Why don't you two go ahead?"

"Okay, I'll talk to you soon. And I'll be in. Really, I will. Soon."

"Don't worry. Just enjoy yourself."

"We will. Come on, Nick. We've got a date with Trombone Shorty."

"Yowza."

"Yowza. Is he a nut or what?"

"Or what," I responded as they linked arms and trotted off down the street.

I swear, that night at the Kingfish must have set off a hormone explosion the likes of which had never been seen before. Nick and Maggie were mating like rabbits. Mike and Monique were acting very strangely—although maybe I was just reading into that. And Cindy…

Cindy had become the belle of Berkeley while Biff had lost any semblance of self-confidence. Naturally, it had not happened with just that one night, but after a few weeks of ego-battering, he succumbed. And Cindy just grew stronger. She began to see her self-worth as including more than just being Biff's girlfriend.

I saw her here sporadically. Actually, maybe that was why Kevin was here—hoping to catch a glimpse of her. She was working just around the corner at the Edible Complex and living in an apartment with a friend while Biff had moved home after graduation. Amazingly enough, they still saw each other. Cindy claimed she was still in love with Biff, but the tables had definitely turned. Biff had become very possessive while Cindy managed to flirt with just about every guy she came into contact with. It was still not the healthiest relationship, in my opinion, but at this point, an opinion was all I had to offer.

I figured I had done enough pondering for the day and was packing up to leave when Mike stopped by.

"Hey, Kat. Seen that new guy—what's his name—Leonard?"

Kat. I hated that. It really didn't take much effort to add the second syllable to Kathy.

"No, Mike I haven't."

"Shit."

"What's the problem?"

"Well, you know, he's the guy that kept sending the ultimatums to his girlfriend in the form of an Instagram quiz with corresponding pictures. Remember? A. We can continue as we are. B. We can become engaged. C. We can be friends for life? Remember?"

"Yeah."

"Well, I'm supposed to be helping him with the assertiveness stuff, but I lost him."

"What were you doing to help him with his assertiveness?"

"I had him working out with the guys on the rugby field."

"You had Leonard, 130-pound Leonard, out with those animals?"

"Yeah. So?"

"I'm afraid we may never see him again."

"Nah, Lenny is tough. You'll see. I'll whip him into shape."

"Uh huh."

"Speaking of shape, have you seen Kiki?" Again with the nicknames.

"I think Monique said she'd be in her office."

"Office, yeah, okay."

"What do you need her for?"

"Nothing. Business. You know. Business."

Mike raced off to campus. I still couldn't quite figure out what was going on with them but was mostly just glad they weren't mad at Maggie and me for not showing up for that first meeting after the night at the Kingfish. Maggie had been so rattled with the Nick stuff she forgot to go and forgot to tell me to go. Mostly, I had to thank the stars they weren't at each other's throats anymore. I was having a dinner party later that week to toast the success of the Council, and I didn't want any flying silverware.

Chapter Seventeen
MIKE

My babe. I gotta tell ya, she was one hot tamale. The more I got to know Monique—Kiki I got to calling her; it made her a little nuts but was easier on the mouth than Monique—the more I realized that, wow, this woman was just so… hot. I mean, all of her was hot. Not just her bod, although her bod really sizzled.

No, it was her mind. The way she had of looking at life. The way she crinkled her nose in disgust when I disagreed with her about something. The crazy ass words she used. Mostly, though, it was the way that underneath that Hard Ass exterior she was a marshmallow—a big lovable marshmallow with the best bazoongas this side of anywhere. Sorry. Sue me. I'm a guy.

I was surprised to learn that we'd both had parents who divorced when we were young. There's kind of a kindred spirit among those of us from, you know, "broken" homes. Not that it's that unusual these days. Still, it's like we understood each other as we endured the same shit. We've endured our families being destroyed and our parents acting like fucking children is what we've endured.

I remember how pissed off I was with my Dad. What a yutz. I was 14. He was 52 and suddenly decided he liked the 25-year-old cashier at the A&P better than my mom. It was so fucking tacky. And embarrassing. I mean, here was my Dad acting like a horny teenager. He even bought a Corvette and started dying his hair—the full horror.

The only thing I give my Dad credit for was letting my mom go quickly. He was honest enough to move out and divorce her when he took up Priscilla. (Yes, Priscilla. The worst, right?) My mom cried her eyes out, and for months, my sisters and I took turns listening to her and comforting her. So, my Mom cried her eyes out, and then, realizing the shithead wasn't coming back, she got a job and her real estate license and made big bucks selling real estate in Connecticut. Go figure, right? Dad and Priscilla were divorced four years later, and mom became the local celebrity realtor.

That was when I realized that you get what you give. You know? You get what you give.

Kiki had it a lot worse. For one, I had my sisters, and she was all alone, an only kid. Also, her dad started fooling around on her mom ten years before he left. Didn't tell her mom about the other woman but did tell her to her face that he didn't love her—that he felt warmly toward her (can you believe that shit? warmly?)—but did not love her. For ten years, that woman did everything she could to make him love her, and he still left. Kiki blames them both in a way: her dad for being too weak to leave when he wasn't happy and her mom for playing the victim and not moving on with her life.

From what Kiki told me, they fought like hell over who would get her and still barely speak. Kiki had to make appointments to visit each of them separately on holidays. I swear, if I get ahold of them someday, I'm gonna slap them silly for what they did to my babycakes.

I found Kiki where Kathy said she'd be: office hours. I had to smile as even though she was only teaching one course during summer school, there were half a dozen dudes snaking down the hall waiting to talk to her.

I signaled to her that I was outside. She nodded, an officious kinda nod. We'd decide to keep things between us quiet. See, we both agreed it was just physical, and that at some point it would burn out, so we thought it would only complicate things if anybody knew about us.

Well, Connor knew about us, mostly because he'd walked in on us when we were doing it in the equipment room. After our first night in the War Council offices, we were kind of into the danger thing. Still, other than Connor—who said he'd keep it on the QT—we met on the sly.

Finally, Kiki shooed the last of her male admirers out of her office and stood at the door, waiting for me with her sternest look plastered on her face. Whoosh. Total babe.

"Coach Banks. What can I do for you?"

"Well, Professor DeVillier, it's like this…"

"Excuse my manners. Why don't you come in, Coach Banks, so we can speak more privately?"

I entered the office. "Thank you, Professor DeVillier. See, it's like this: Some of my players have been complaining about your, uh, workload, and I thought we might discuss lightening it a bit."

"Hmmm." She closed the door. "Well now, Coach Banks, I might see my way clear to lightening the load, as you put it, but well, it depends."

She locked the door.

"Depends?"

"On what inducements you might offer."

"Inducements?"

"Strip."

"I'm sorry?"

"You heard me."

"Gee, Professor DeVillier. Well, okay…"

As I took my clothes off, Kiki looked at me with her most fiendish grin—oh how I loved that grin.

"You may take my clothes off now." She stood up and stuck out her arms like a scarecrow. She looked ridiculous and seemed to be about to bust up laughing. I started unbuttoning her dress.

"Snappy frock."

"Shut up and take it off."

Once it fell to the ground, I grabbed her and threw her on the couch. She screamed with delight—shit, I hope it was delight.

"Oh baby."

"Indeed."

We smothered each other with kisses and rolled onto the carpet.

"Wait, rug burn."

Remembering the pain we'd experienced after our first night at the War Council offices, Kiki grabbed a chenille blanket from the couch and laid it on the carpet.

"Is that new?"

"A necessary accoutrement."

Then she pounced.

"Hey, I wanna be on top."

"You were on top last time."

"Yeah, but it's my fantasy."

"All right. Fine."

She rolled over, and I looked deep into her eyes.

"Oh, Coach Banks…"

"Say it."

"No."

"Say it."

"Really?" She rolled her eyes at me.

"Please?"

After a beat, she quietly said: "Go Cal."

"Again."

A little louder: "Go Cal."

"That's the ticket." I smiled.

"Go Cal. Go Cal." She smiled. "Oh, Go Cal."

Soon I'd answered with a rather vibrant "Go Cal" of my own, and we were lying on the newly acquired "accoutrement" in each other's arms.

"That was splendiferous."

"That it was, baby. I sure love... this."

She looked over at me, her eyes glowing. "Yes."

A moment passed, and we both sighed, still happily locked together. Luckily, we knew it was just physical and would burn out someday.

"So... about that workload."

She smiled. "Can't. Up for tenure this year." Then she laughed. "I can't believe we just did it in my office!"

"Pfft. It's summer. No one is ever on campus after two. Besides, they'll just figure you've got the game on in here."

"Yeah, sure, the game." She smiled. Kiki smiled. Oh, how I loved that smile.

Later we both fell asleep, and I woke up just as the sun was beginning to set behind one of other buildings on campus. An orange glow filled the room, Kiki's office, her home base, her life. I looked around at her books and her papers scattered about and at her lying peacefully in my arms. This woman could make me feel like nothing else. Nothing else.

Thank God it was just physical.

Chapter Eighteen
CINDY

P ower. I must admit I was still kinda confused about what Maggie meant when she kept talking about the role of power in love and relationships. I mean, well, the night at the Kingfish was pretty weird, you know? Still, it took me awhile to figure out what it all meant.

I will admit that having all those guys totally into me that night was really cool. But I was also pretty pissed off that fuckface Biff was slathering all over Professor DeVillier—Monique. It stabbed at my insides is what it did. I just didn't get it. If we were so great together, why did he lust after her? Why would he risk what we had for a roll in the hay with a sleaze like Kitty or a hard ass like Monique? I mean, I knew it was an act with Monique, but the asshole was buying it!

I tried not to think about it and concentrated on Connor, the Australian guy, beside me. I mean, he was cute, and big. Biff was a scrawny little matchstick beside Connor. And Connor had this curly brown hair with brown eyes and tanned skin and that cool accent. Like right out of a movie.

He seemed to like me, Connor did. I knew that Coach Banks had, well, bartered their participation. Connor told me that Coach had cut laps for all those who'd help out. The other guys seemed to feel it was, you know, a lark and just partied, but Connor really seemed sincere. I mean, he told me what was up. That was worth something, wasn't it? And he said he was surprised how cute I was and even asked me to go out with him after we left the bar. I told him he didn't have to, but he said he wanted to. He liked me, right?

We ended up walking around Berkeley for a couple hours. We watched the weirdos on Telegraph and stopped in every bar along the street to see who had the best drinks—kinda like a progressive dinner, you know? And we talked. Mostly Connor talked about rugby. He was really passionate about rugby and seemed to feel that rugby was like this microcosm of life and that each game represented the struggle that is life. I wasn't sure how guys pummeling each other over possession of a ball represented life, but he seemed to buy it so who was I to argue? Boys, right?

After a while, we walked up to the I-House where he lived. Funny, I'd walked past the building the four years I'd been at Berkeley and had never been inside. I mentioned that to Connor, and he asked me in.

Okay, I know what you're thinking now, so I'll tell you: We did it. Okay? It was weird, you know? There I was, so pissed off at Biff, who until recently I had thought would be the only man in my life forever. He was off fucking around with skanks—not Professor DeVillier but Kitty and the countless others I now knew existed—and there was Connor, hot as can be. I gotta admit I was pretty psyched by the attention.

We went up to his room, and he put on some music. We were sitting there listening to, I think it was Bruno Mars, when he kissed me. It was kinda strange. I was sitting there kissing him, and all these weird thoughts kept swooshing through my brain. On the one hand I felt "ha, I'm getting Biff the fuckface back." On the other hand, I felt guilty, like I was betraying the fuckface, mostly because he'd always really liked the fact that he was my first, you know. And I liked the fact that he liked that, until he started humping anything that moved. Fuckface asshole.

I also felt a little like I was using Connor, but he didn't really seem to care and he was awfully cute and really seemed to like me. Okay, so we're still kissing, and now I'm trying to figure out what I'm feeling. I was thinking how different it was kissing Connor from kissing Biff and how awkward that first time kissing somebody is. You know how it is: When you've been with some-body for a while, your lips know right where to go while the first time you kiss somebody, you keep missing and fumbling, and it's just a little weird.

Next thing I know we're, like, out of our clothes and, you know, and I guess the first thing I notice is that Connor is, you know, a big guy, all over. The rest was kind of a blur. To tell you the truth, it was all kind of a blur: the Kingfish, that night, sleeping with Connor… And the next morning was just plain freaky. Mostly because, I don't know, I felt closer to Connor all of a sudden, you know? I mean, I'd slept in his massive arms all night, and I felt warm and protected the way I did with Biff. Only it wasn't Biff. It was Connor, and I didn't really know Connor. He was just this big cute guy with a neat accent who loved rugby and Biff was who I thought I would spend the rest of my life with. How could I feel these things?

"It's natural," Maggie said when she heard my story later that week.

Maggie, Monique, Kathy, and Hallie were meeting with me at the War Council offices while planning their next assault on Biff. The guys weren't there. I think they'd sent them away so they could see me alone. You know, gal talk. I was glad because I needed some advice, bad, and the gals in the sorority wouldn't understand. I spilled my guts.

"I feel kinda, you know, guilty, like I'm as bad as he is."

"You didn't make the rules, honey; he did. You're just living by them," Monique said.

"Besides, it's healthy. No one should marry the first person they sleep with."

"Oh, come on, Monique. Don't be so cynical," Kathy said. "I did."

"No way."

"Really?" Hallie piped in.

"What?"

"Didn't you ever, you know, wonder?" Monique asked.

"No."

"Really?"

"What? You think that's weird? Hallie?" Kathy seemed to be looking for support.

"I'd been with my share of jerks before Randy came along. It made me realize what a gem I had."

"Well, maybe I knew I had a gem without having to comparison shop."

"Oooo."

"A bit defensive, aren't we?" Maggie asked.

"No."

"Listen, Cindy," Maggie turned to me, "except for Kathy here who, I think we can all agree, is practically perfect in every way—yes, Mary Poppins is her patron saint..."

Everybody but Kathy snickered.

"...most of us need to grow a bit before we're ready to decide who we want to spend our lives with. We need to realize our power."

"See, that's what confuses me. This power stuff."

"Well, you mentioned wondering why Biff would risk your relationship to sleep with other women. Why do you think he would do that?"

"I don't know."

"Because to him it's not much of a risk," Monique answered.

"What do you mean?"

"He expected you to be there waiting for him," Maggie said.

"Just like I have been every time before." What a wuss I was.

"Exactly."

"But if he loves me, why would he do something that hurts me?"

"Ah, the egocentric male," Monique said.

"Ahem," Hallie interrupted.

"Yes, there are exceptions," said Monique. "And we're talking generalizations here, but most men are socialized to be rather egocentric creatures. They don't change because they hurt someone else—they don't *realize* they're hurting someone else. They change when it hurts them."

"They're like dogs," said Kathy, finally getting into it. "You've got to punish the behavior."

"Kathy!" Maggie said.

"What?"

"You punish Brian?"

"Subtly," she said. "I didn't get this degree in psychology for nothing."

"I'd like to take this analogy a step further, if I could," Monique said.

Uh oh.

"Think of men as big sloppy drooling dogs," she began. "They're cute, they're fuzzy, they're incredibly lovable, and they give great big sloppy kisses. But they also run in circles without thinking, and frankly, sometimes need to have their noses shoved in a little shit before they learn not to do it in the house."

"I've found that in a lot of ways they don't think in the logical progressions we do," said Hallie. "It's not that he deliberately sets out to hurt you; he just doesn't see the effect, period."

"Let me give you an example of that," Kathy said. "One day, when our kids were toddlers, Brian put a full glass of water on our coffee table and left the room. Our toddlers were in there. Toddlers are very mobile. So, I said, 'Brian, how could you leave that on the table with them in the room?' It never occurred to him. His entire thought process was: I want to put this down. Here is a table."

"And that's how they can be with sex," Monique said. "They've got this external organ that says, 'I want that,' and they act without thinking. Then it's like, 'what have I done?'"

I was still confused. "But how can they separate sex from the feelings it brings?"

"Oh please." Monique practically choked on her coffee. "Guys could do it in a pail if they wanted."

They all laughed.

"Just look at their sex organs," Maggie pointed out. "It's outside them. It's inside us. They can separate. We—well, most of us female types—can't."

"Yeah, there are some women who can separate," Hallie said.

Everyone turned to look at Monique.

"What?" Then she got it. "Hey, I feel. I do. I am not the Hard Ass everyone thinks I am. I feel. It's one of my weaknesses, okay? Sheesh."

"But there are some women..." Hallie continued.

"Yeah," I agreed. "There are some girls in the house. They talk about it all the time: 'spo-ing.'"

"Spo-ing?"

"Sport sex."

"Oh." They looked at each other with raised eyebrows and mouthed the word.

"The thing to remember," Maggie said, "is the fact that if there is initial interest there, they want us. We start with the power. I mean, it's a visual—well, maybe more visceral—power, that attraction."

"Unfortunately," Monique continued for her, "many women then turn around and throw that power away. They sleep with a guy once, decide he's Prince Charming and toss their identity and self-respect right out the window. Not only is it incredibly demeaning, it doesn't work."

"Doesn't work?"

"Who wants a passive little cupcake slobbering all over them?"

"Yeah, ever see those girls carrying tins of cookies over to the fraternity houses? Sickening."

That one opened my eyes a bit. "Oh shit."

"I'm sorry, Cindy, but, well, let's work on this. How did it make you feel to, well, service Biff like that?"

"Service?"

"Sheesh, Monique."

"What? God, you guys. Go on, Cindy."

"Well, I thought I was being nice. That made me feel good. But then it felt bad because I was doing all these nice things for him, and he was kinda being a shit, you know? So then, I thought maybe if I did more, I wouldn't lose him."

"So, you felt out of control and desperate not to lose him?" Kathy asked.

"Right."

"Wrong."

"Appeasement never works," Hallie added. "Didn't work in World War II, and it doesn't work in love."

"Cindy, did you ever think that maybe you weren't allowing him to give?" Kathy asked.

"Huh?"

"If you are running around giving all the time, people don't have room to give back. You have to allow people to give by taking a little."

"And then you won't be taken for granted," Maggie said.

"It's a principle of human nature that we like what we have to work for. You're not allowing Biff to feel that," Kathy said.

"Did you ever notice that sometimes it's the bitchiest women who have the nicest husbands?" Maggie asked.

"Let's lose the word bitchy, shall we?" Monique suggested.

"Toughest?" Hallie offered.

"Straight shooters. Self-fulfilled women who know what they want. Indifference kills," Monique said.

Kathy turned to me. "Cindy, we're not saying you have to be a bitch, but you do need to build up your life outside of Biff. Get out from this spell he has you under. Connor was a good step, but let's keep it going. Enjoy your life. Maybe Biff will become a part of that life, but he should never be all of it. You should never lose all of yourself in a relationship. Then no matter who you are with or not with, you will be happier—because you will have you. You will respect yourself, and you will like yourself, and others will be drawn to that strength. That's the power."

I noticed that Maggie seemed to be listening to Kathy's words as much as I was. Hold onto yourself and you will have power. Huh.

The next few weeks everything changed. I guess you could say I grew up a little bit. I started looking at my relationships with men differently. I mean, why should I limit my life until I was ready to settle down, get married, whatever? Sheesh, I was a free agent.

I decided not to sleep with anyone else until I figured out who or what it was I really wanted.

Too confusing. Biff and I had been broken up since that night I found him with Kitty at the Kingfish. And now that I knew that I would, you know, bond with whoever I slept with, I decided to keep myself clear headed. Besides, it was much more fun to flirt. I loved having a pack o' guys and spending time with all of them.

After graduation, I started working at the Edible Complex and moved in with Bunny. I wasn't real sure what direction I wanted to go in—grad school or entry-level job—and I certainly didn't want to go home, so I decided to stay in Berkeley and take some time to think about it.

It seemed like suddenly there were guys everywhere. My pack o' guys included Kevin, who I kept running into at Café Strada, and Connor, who I hung out with at the I-House and went running with. He'd been real understanding about why I wanted to keep things platonic for awhile. Like I said, he was pretty easygoing. He continued suggesting he'd be up for more, and we kissed every once in a while, and I have to admit it was tough staying away from him 'cuz I kinda missed the sex, but I did, for now.

And Biff. Biff stopped by the Edible Complex every once in a while. The War Council had really skewered his self-confidence. In a way, though, it turned him into a much nicer person.

Naturally, the night at the Kingfish didn't immediately change his ways, so the War Council continued their attack on his ego. They had me turn down all his requests for dates, they hacked into his phone and erased his voicemails and texts, and they passed a rumor around the sororities that he had a communicable disease. It was pretty awful for him, and I began to feel a little sorry for him. Monique's puppy dog image came to mind every time he came by to visit me at work. He really did look like a dog who'd had his nose rubbed in some shit.

It was mid-summer by the time he hit rock bottom. One day, he stopped by the Edible Complex and seemed particularly determined.

"Hi."

"Hi, Biff."

"Listen, I've got something important to talk to you about. Can I stop by this evening?"

"Tonight?"

"Yeah."

I looked at those puppy dog eyes. "Yeah, okay."

He got all excited and ran off.

Later that night, he arrived at my doorstep all dressed up. No Budweiser suit but he looked good. He was carrying a bottle of champagne and a dozen roses. Can you believe that?

"Hi, Biff. What's up?"

"Can I come in?"

"Well, sure."

We sat down. My roommates, Bunny and Jane, were out, so we were alone.

"Listen, Cindy, I, um, realize I've been some-what of a shit and all..."

"Yes. Yes, you have."

"I know. But, well, it seems to me that we meant a lot to each other once, and maybe we could again."

"Maybe."

"That's why I was hoping that you could consider, well, I know it's what you wanted at one time, and now it's what I want..."

I looked at him—what the fuck was he talking about? He got this determined look on his face and slipped off the couch to awkwardly balance on one knee.

"Cindy, will you marry me?"

The puppy dog eyes gazed up at me imploringly. Shit. I was shocked outta my socks. This was the moment I had been dreaming of for three years: Biff fuckface the Fifth was begging me to marry him. I felt this incredibly surge of, well, now that you mention it: power.

Chapter Nineteen
NICK

False happiness.

Have you ever had everything in your life going so well that you knew it was not destined to last? Everything so perfect that you knew it was an illusion? That with one false move it would all come crashing down around you like a house of cards? Well, I was living in a house of cards that summer in Berkeley.

Not to be melodramatic. Ah, hell, what's wrong with a little melodrama? I was in love, and love is melodramatic. I mean, really, if you can't be melodramatic when you're in love, when can you?

So, there I was, in love with Maggie, in love with the most incredible creature on the face of the earth (note the melodrama). And she was in love with me. That was the miraculous part. Maggie had actually fallen in love with me. But our love was built on a lie—a manipulation, a trap.

It wouldn't have been so bad if it had just been me who had manipulated her. I could tell her the lengths I'd gone to in order to get her to notice me, and we would laugh and kiss and tell our grandchildren all about it. But no, it was not just me. I had turned her friends against her. God, what a beast I was.

Still, in my defense, it was Maggie and that whole damn logic thing that had started it all. Logic. Ha! Love and logic. Trying to insert logic into love is a completely illogical task. Because love is not logical. It does not follow the rules of logic. We fall in love at the wrong times with the wrong people, and there's nothing we can do about it. That's the beauty of it all. They're not the wrong people because we love them, and it's not the wrong time if we're capable of falling in love.

I was in love—real love—for the first time in my life. I was 37 years old and acting like a stupid teenager. I swear, I thought I'd have an acne breakout at any moment. Nothing in my life had prepared me for the totality of Maggie or how she made me feel. I would lie awake watching her sleep and felt a happiness pervade my being like nothing I had experienced before.

My feelings for Maggie made me realize how detached I'd been in my past relationships. Not that I didn't care for those women. I did, but it always felt more like a research project. I enjoyed getting to know them but never felt my soul being opened the way I did with Maggie.

I wanted to give her so much. With the other women, it was like they always wanted more than I could give. I felt they impinged on my freedom, and when they pressured for more, I left. Simple. Troubling but simple.

Finally, I was with a woman who made me want to chuck my freedom right out of the window. I wasn't afraid of losing my freedom. I was a little afraid that I wasn't afraid, and I was afraid of the effect she had on me. But what I was really afraid of was the fact that I might lose these feelings.

False happiness.

Are we meant to enjoy a present so fabulous, so wondrous, so spectacular but with no thought of a future? Can we live in a bubble without a thought as to the moment when reality will poke its ugly head in and destroy it? I don't know. I certainly wasn't feeling capable of it. I kept wondering if maybe real misery would be better than the precarious false happiness I found myself in.

But I still couldn't bring myself to tell Maggie about the AWAC's involvement in the beginning of our relationship. How could I tell her that so many of my early moves had been dictated by a team? That we'd plotted over butterflied lamb and scalloped potatoes at Kathy's house? That her best friends in the world thought so little of her that they didn't trust her to fall in love on her own?

Every time Maggie and I were together, I ached to tell her, ached to confess my part and to tell her that it was because I loved her that I was desperate enough to use drastic measures, to use her friends—her methods—against her. Wouldn't she see that it was only because we loved her that we'd wanted to help her? That we'd only used the ideas that she was so vigorously promoting? That it's not that we went behind her back to embarrass her but to help her? Wouldn't she understand that?

Would you?

I might have believed that Maggie would understand the AWAC and our intentions if she had remained as passionate about the War Council as she was in the beginning. But she wasn't. It wasn't long after our first night together that Maggie began to lose interest in the War Council. And, to make matters worse, she kept saying how great it was that we didn't need something like the War Council. That we'd come together naturally. That the War Council was only for truly dysfunctional people—pathetic, she called them—pathetically dysfunctional people unable to express their feelings naturally. That we were lucky because it was so "natural" the way we had fallen in love. Ugh. What was I to do?

I had a month to go before making my final decision about Paris. For the first time, I didn't want to go on one of my adventures. I was finally in love with a woman I didn't want to leave, but I was desperately afraid that she would leave me. Upon reflection, I suppose I shouldn't have worried so much about how or when my house of cards would fall down about me because, as often happens in life, although we may think we are prepared for the inevitable, it is still a shock to the system when it happens.

The moment of my destruction came, ironically enough, at another dinner at Kathy and Brian's house in the city. I should have known. Life is often cruel in dealing us our fates. Much as my father dropped dead just as his dream was about to become a reality, I was about to lose my true love at the site of not only our first meeting—when I gazed into those passionate eyes for the first time—but of my most callous betrayal. To this day, I am unable to eat butterflied lamb or scalloped potatoes.

Luckily, Kathy was not serving butterflied lamb this evening. She had put together some sort of whitefish in creme sauce and a light tomato salad with summer greens. With the bottles of sauvignon blanc we were providing, the meal was going to be scrumptious. I suppose if I had to choose a setting for my destruction, it was nice to have it be so civilized. Not all battlefields are ugly, not all scars visible. Sorry—got a little carried away with the melodrama again.

The whole evening played out like a gothic opera—Kathy and Brian were even playing the classic three tenors on Spotify: Pavarotti, Carreras, and Domingo singing the great arias. Music. The power of their voices reminded me of Maggie and the important role music had played in our relationship. We had been making our way through a wide variety of music, all of which made our time together amazing. What would I do without this woman? I had to hope she would come to understand.

As the sun began to set, it created an orange glow to Kathy's living room. I looked over at Maggie taking a sip of wine and laughing at something Brian said. She looked over at me and smiled. Her eyes sparkled. It was one of those moments when a wave of pure feeling invaded my body.

Suddenly, Kathy burst into the room from the kitchen.

"I have news!"

Everyone looked up.

"War Council news."

Brian, Hallie, Randy, and Maggie stopped talking, put down their drinks, and turned to listen.

"Wait, where are Mike and Monique?"

"They went to put away their coats."

"Can you believe how cold the city's been this summer?" Hallie asked, perhaps attempting to fill the time until Mike and Monique returned.

"I know," Brian said. "We went to an outdoor concert Sunday afternoon, and people were wearing mittens. Mittens in August for God's sake."

"We say this every year," Randy said. "It's always cold in August in the city."

"That's true. Luckily, Berkeley's been better. At least ten degrees warmer," Kathy said. "How long do you think they're going to take?"

"I'll go get them," I offered.

I walked down the hall and went to open the door to the master bedroom, where everyone had been putting their coats. It opened a crack, then bumped into something pressed up against the door. I then heard a voice say: "Go Cal."

"What are you guys doing? Are you watching the game?"

"Yeah," Mike said. "Sorry. We'll be right out."

"Okay." That was weird. I didn't think that football season had started. Before I could ponder further, I got back to the living room, and they all turned to look at me. "They'll be right out."

"So, what's the news?"

"Just wait."

Mike came into the living room, followed shortly after by Monique.

"All right, what's the emergency?" Monique asked.

"I have some big news," said Kathy.

Mike and Monique chose seats on opposite sides of the room but continued to exchange glances. I think that's what they were doing, anyway. Rumors had been circulating about them and their behavior just now was pretty odd, but maybe I was reading too much into it.

"Maggie should really be the one to tell you this, but I just checked the messages at the War Council offices."

"And...?" Maggie asked.

"Biff proposed to Cindy last night."

"Oh my God."

"The little prick finally succumbed."

"Is she going to marry him?"

"I don't know. In the message she just said he'd asked."

"I hope she leaves him at the altar," said Monique.

Mike smiled. "Either way, this calls for a celebration." He raised his glass. "To victory for our first War Council client.'

"Not really our first," Hallie said. "Not if you count Maggie."

"What?" Maggie asked.

A brisk wind began heading toward my house of cards.

"Didn't Nick tell you? He used the War Council—or the anti-War Council I think we called it—to get to know you."

Maggie's eyes turned to me but instead of offering the pure guileless affection of a few minutes ago, it was like a door had slammed shut. Her eyes looked like stone, and her face showed the betrayal she felt. The eyes I had finally opened, the soul I had finally entered, the love I had finally awakened—all closed and in one brief terrifying moment were snatched from my grasp.

My house of cards fell down around me that glorious summer evening in the city by the bay. Merde.

Chapter Twenty
MAGGIE

Success. I was a fucking success. I had proven everything I'd set out to prove: that the War Council could work, that love could be logical, that even I would fall for logic and manipulation and mistake it for love. So why did I want to puke?

There I was, surrounded by my friends, by the man I'd fallen in love with—or thought I'd fallen in love with—feeling better about my life than I had in years. And then they told me the whole thing was a joke. I was a joke. My feelings were a joke. I had proven Kathy wrong, and yet somehow I was the one with egg on my face.

How could they do this to me? How could they think so little of me that they would go behind my back like that? I felt so betrayed by the thought of them conspiring and discussing my love life behind my back. My life. Who were they to decide how my life should be run? Suddenly I wondered how I could have believed in these people. All of them. How I could have opened myself up and… trusted them. I felt like such a fucking idiot. And how could I have thought that I loved Nick when it was all just a manipulation?

I don't want you to think I was uncivilized in my response to their betrayal. After Hallie spilled the beans about the—what did they call it?—oh yes, the Anti-War Council War Council Conspiracy or AWAC. Cute. So glad they were having such fun at my expense. Anyway, after she spilled the beans, I looked over at Nick. I just couldn't believe he had lied to me like that. I had trusted him. But there it was written all over his face—shock, embarrassment, maybe a little bit of relief. He gave me a weak smile; I suppose to try and make me feel better. Shithead. I had pictures of them all laughing and plotting to help poor pitiful dysfunctional Maggie find love. What a bunch of assholes.

But no, I kept my cool and plastered a smile on my face. "Well, now, isn't this a surprise," I said. "I guess you got me."

"Maggie, don't be like that," Kathy said. "We only did it to help you."

Kathy. Perfect Kathy that nothing ever bothers, with her perfect husband and two perfect children. Why can't we all be like perfect perfect Kathy who throws great dinner parties and betrays her friends behind their backs?

"Don't worry, Kathy. I won't ruin your party. But if you will all excuse me, I have to use the bathroom."

I again gave them my best "fuck you" smile and left the room. I could hear Mike and Monique asking what was going on. Oh, so they weren't in on it. Well, I could see it was a very select little clique that was involved in betraying me.

Because I have never been good at coming up with snappy comebacks on the spot and because I felt like punching something, and although they deserved it, I didn't want to start punching any one of them, I decided it was best that I get out of there as quickly as possible. So, I walked past the bathroom, stopped in the master bedroom to pick up my coat—it had become rather chilly outside after all—and headed out the front door. I could hear everyone yelling at me to come back, but I kept on walking. I wanted to get as far away as quickly as possible.

"Maggie, Maggie, don't go."

It was Nick. He was running after me. I kept walking.

"Maggie, talk to me."

"I see you are continuing to play your part rather convincingly, Nick."

"Maggie, it wasn't an act."

"Yeah, sure. Why don't you go back to your little AWAC club, Nick? They're obviously the people you want to be with."

"Please don't do this, Maggie. I am so sorry for not telling you, but I was afraid of losing you."

"Yeah, well, too late, huh?"

"Please don't be like this."

"You're starting to sound like Kathy. Don't be like what? Like hurt? Like betrayed? Like wondering how I could have possibly thought I was in love with a man who could do this to me? Gee, I'm so sorry, Nick. How would you like me to act? You want me to be like perfect stoic Kathy who never feels a thing? Who sails through life without once losing her temper?"

"No. I don't want you to be like Kathy," he said. "Kathy doesn't have your passion. And I don't love Kathy. I love you."

"Yeah, well, you have a funny way of showing it." I tried walking faster, anything to shake him.

"Maggie, please don't run off. Let's talk about this."

"I don't want to talk, Nick. I want to run. I want to run as far away from you and my so-called friends and the fucking War Council and these horrible wrenchingly painful feelings as I can. I want to run from you, Nick, because at the moment you represent pain. I don't see love when I look at you; I see pain. So, please, if you care about me, stop following me."

I kept walking and after a few moments of silence, Nick stopped. I only looked back once. That was a mistake. I saw the sorrow painted all over his face. His blue eyes—those beautiful blue eyes that had opened me to what I thought was love—looked hollow and sad. For a brief instant, I thought about turning back, but then the image of them all sitting around laughing and plotting took over. What was planned, Nick? Was this planned? The sorrowful eyes? Did Kathy tell you to come out and play sad to get me back? Was this a manipulation, too? Shit. Would I ever trust again?

It took me three buses, BART, and a 15-minute walk from the station to get back to my apartment in Berkeley. I was still mad, and all the snappy comebacks that I'd been unable to come up with at the time were now buffeting around my head.

"Oh yeah, you and what army?" I should've said. Or "No, you're the loser!" Or maybe just a slap across the jaw. Haven't you always dreamed of that? Just boof, a smack across the ole shinola. My problem was who to hit. Nick? Kathy? The whole lot of them? I suppose I could let Mike and Monique off the hook because they weren't in on it. And why? Was my case not worthy of them? Nah, I'd take them all on, the whole lot of them. They'd be sorry they ever crossed me. They'd be sorry.

The anger was starting to wear off as I let myself into my apartment. Unfortunately, it was followed by profound sadness. Was I pathetic or what? What was wrong with me? Why couldn't I just fall in love like other people? Why was my love life so complicated? Why did I fall in love with men who couldn't be there for me? Why did they always leave? I mean, let's face it, even if I forgave Nick, what was the point? He was leaving for Paris soon.

I slumped onto my couch and pulled out my phone. I had turned it off on the bus to stop the incessant buzzing each time a text came in—from them—and, after pondering it a moment, decided to turn it back on. The texts and voicemails immediately started popping up. I ignored the texts as they all seemed to say "call me" and mindlessly started listening to the voicemails.

"Maggie, it's Nick. Please talk to me. At least let me know you that you got home safely. Please call me. Please. Okay, I'll try later."

Delete.

"Maggie, it's Kathy. Come on. Don't be such a pill. We only did this to help you. And you should know that Nick refused to talk to us after you two got together. I swear. It's been real, Maggie. The love has been real. Please don't blame him. It's all me. I've been a real shit, and I'm sorry. Please call me."

Delete.

"Maggie, it's Monique. I have now heard the whole story and just have to say it's abominable what they did to you. I think you should know that Mike and I really lit into them. Abhorrent. Their actions were abhorrent, but they are repenting. And, Maggie, I'd just like to leave you with this one piece of advice: Men are dogs, Maggie. Men are dogs."

In the background, I heard Mike saying, "What's that? Men? Dogs?"

"Shh. I'll explain later. Bye, Maggie. Call me if you need to talk."

Okay, so Monique's message brought a wee smile to my face. I wouldn't sock her in the face when I did the others. As I was deleting the message, another call was coming in. I didn't recognize the number but figured they wouldn't stop until I answered and let them know I was home, so I answered.

"What?"

"Maggie?"

My heart skipped a beat.

"Hello? Maggie?"

I knew this voice. It wasn't Nick. It wasn't Kathy. It wasn't Monique.

It was a voice I hadn't heard in three years.

Three years of fantasy and memories and occasional emails and texts and suddenly I was faced with the reality of his voice.

"Hello? Do I have the right number? Maggie?"

"Uh, Bill?" Bill! It was Bill.

"Yeah. Maggie. Wow. Your voice sounds great. It's been a long time."

Silence. What do I say? A long time? A long time? It's been three years. What do you say after three years? What's up? What's been up for three years? It was like talking to a stranger and yet a stranger that I knew, a stranger who was able to conjure up feelings I thought had died, a stranger who could still make my heart beat faster, my mouth go dry, and the earth stand still.

"Yeah, so, Bill. A long time. It has been a long time. So, uh, what's up?" Okay, I said it. Really, what else do you say?

"Well, actually, I'm, well, I'm coming to Berkeley."

"You're coming to Berkeley?" I sat up but held myself back from sounding excited. He'd said he was going to visit a number of times in texts and emails over the years and never materialized.

"Yeah, I have a plane ticket for the 8th?"

Ticket? He actually had a ticket?

"You arrive on the 8th? 8th of what?"

"Well, um, August."

"August? That's next week."

"Yeah, I know it's short notice, but the wire service just gave me the time off." Silence. "I'd, uh, like to see you if it's okay."

"Uh huh."

"We have a lot to talk about."

"Uh huh."

Like what? What do you want to talk about, Bill?

"Listen, Maggie, I know it's late there so, well, I'll let you go. I'll call again to let you know when exactly I'll be getting to Berkeley, okay?"

"Yeah, great."

"Great. Maggie, I can't tell you how good it feels to hear your voice and know that I'm going to be seeing you soon." Silence. "I've, uh, missed you," he said.

"Uh huh," I squeaked.

"Talk to you soon. Bye." And with that the call ended.

I put my phone down. At least, that's what I think I did. I was so spaced that I wasn't really in control of my actions.

Bill. After all these years. Bill. Coming here. Coming to see me. And he said he missed me, and from the tone of his voice, I could tell there was still something there. Dammit.

I must admit that the first thought that came to mind was "Ha!" to all the naysayers like Kathy who said he'd never come back. He was coming back. So, ha! I jumped up and began dancing around the apartment. Bill missed me, and he's coming back. Ha!

Then it began to sink in. He's coming back. The man who had been living as a fantasy in my mind for three years was coming back. What would it be like? What would he be like? Would I still love him? Would he still love me? What if he brought out all the old feelings and then left again? Or what if none of the old feelings were there and the memories of what we had three years ago were destroyed?

I slumped back down into the couch. Shit. What would I do now?

Chapter Twenty-One
NICK

I was dumped. No two ways about it. Dumped. Yep, Maggie dumped me. And I have to admit, it was a whole new experience for me.

Maggie admitted that she was over the "betrayal," as she still chose to call it, that she realized I had only the best intentions—and really I did. I mean, you know I did, right?

But I had two strikes against me. One, I hadn't told her the truth. Even though she understood my "betrayal" (a word that still made me cringe), she didn't understand why I had lied—"by omission" she kept saying. That if we were so close, we should have been able to be honest with one another. That even though she probably still "cared" about me… Cared. Ugh. Strike me down if I ever utter that word to a woman again.

That's probably why it bothered me so much. I was on the receiving end of one of my own speeches. Anyway, she said that even though she probably still "cared" about me, she wouldn't be able to trust me. That was another cringe-worthy word: trust. Dig at my soul, woman.

The other strike against me was a lot more powerful: Bill. Bill was back and he had moved back in with Maggie. Maggie's first love, the one who had been living in her head as a perfect memory for all of these years, was back. The rather precarious present I had been sharing with Maggie was no competition for the perfect memory that Bill represented. So, I had to accept it. I was dumped.

Once my heart and ego had started to recover from the dumping, I realized it was actually a nice feeling. Well, "nice" probably isn't the right word. It's just that there was such a refreshing lack of responsibility that came with being dumped. So, while my first impulse was to run back to all the women I'd dumped in the past and apologize, I then realized they'd gotten off easy. I'd had to walk around feeling responsible and guilty for hurting another human being and wondering if I'd done the right thing. But when you've been dumped, there are no doubts. You had no hand in it. It wasn't your decision. You've been dumped. There it is. Live with it.

So like I said, while my ego was a bit bruised with the brush off and my heart ached with the thought of losing Maggie, I realized that my hands were tied. There was nothing I could do except move on with my life. I wasn't being given any options. It was over. For the first time, it wasn't my doing and that left me free to tackle my next adventure without guilt or recriminations. I had finally fallen in love, but it was not meant to be.

So, my heart said goodbye to Maggie. I knew that I would always love the feelings she had conjured up in me, but I was going to have to move on with my life. Maybe someday we could be together, but for now it was not meant to be. I would leave her to figure things out with Bill, and I would go as scheduled to Paris. I would email and text her fun photos of baguettes and berets, and we could stay friends—an option I'd never really considered with my past girl-friends. It would be great. That was my mantra. I said those words every day until, armed with those thoughts and feelings, I boarded the plane to Paris.

If only the dull aching in my heart would go away.

BILL

Maggie.

What was it about this woman that brought me back after all these years? What was it about the thought of her that had helped me through the three grueling years at the wire service in Tokyo? What was it about her that inspired me to want more from life?

I sat and tried to figure out my feelings for Maggie as I watched her walk up to the podium and prepare to greet her first fall class. It was two weeks before Labor Day, and the fall semester at UC Berkeley was just beginning. Maggie was teaching one of those huge freshman lecture courses: 300 students taking Introduction to Communication Studies. Although her specialty was business communications, she had to teach the introductory course once every couple years. Most professors hate teaching those lower-level courses, but Maggie loved it. She felt it brought her back to her roots. She'd been inspired by one of those courses once and loved giving that back.

I looked around the lecture hall and checked out the students. Most of them were smug little pricks who'd been the top of their classes in high school and thought they knew it all. It was Maggie's job to help them realize that in the big scheme of things they knew nothing and then build them back up to where they were inspired with what knowledge and critical thinking could bring them. Maggie was a master at it. Logical manipulation.

I remembered watching her lecture five years earlier and being awe-inspired then. She was only a teaching assistant at first, leading small discussion sections, but I could see that some-thing about teaching, about knowledge, about learning, inspired the passions inside Maggie.

What was it about this woman that brought me back to her after all these years and continued to inspire me?

I'd always known that what we'd had was special. Sheesh, we both knew it. I mean, I told her often enough. But then I'd left. I knew it had been a blow to Maggie, but she hung in with me while I figured things out with my career and my life. Her emails were wonderful summations of her life in Berkeley and helped me to stay connected to the life I had left. It helped to know that no matter how bad things got, there was Maggie in Berkeley. Those memories sustained me through three stressful workaholic years.

I don't know why I left and didn't feel that I could ask her to come with me, but I couldn't. I loved her enough, but I wasn't ready to take on the responsibility of another human being. It's not that I feel that I have to justify myself, but my life became so complicated after I got my master's. I needed something for myself before I would be ready to really share my life. That's what I told myself anyway.

I hated the thought of losing her, but really, how could I have asked her to just drop her life to follow me when I wasn't even sure what I was looking for? I wasn't really sure who I was and incredibly absorbed in beginning my career so how could I inflict the selfishness associated with that time on another person? Especially Maggie.

Maggie was always so… directed. When we were together, she had gotten to a point where she meshed perfectly with the world she lived in. Her passionate idealism belonged in academia. She was obsessed with how people related to one another, with the illogical nature of our human communication, and how power influences the dynamic. That's why business communications was such a natural fit for her. Maybe I was rationalizing, but I really felt that Maggie belonged here—and I didn't. I did when I was getting my degree. Our timing was perfect then. We were both in school and deeply in love.

I did really love being with her in those days. We balanced each other so well. Maggie saw the small nuances of human existence while I looked at the big: the world and its movements and clashes. I remember getting together with friends and the way Maggie's eyes would light up when we got into a debate on a subject she was passionate about. Passion. Maggie's passion.

In a way, she was the one who helped me realize that it wouldn't be enough for me to stay in the Bay Area. I would have been lost staying put and working for a local publication when what I wanted to do was to see the world, to write about the world, and to delve into its mysteries.

It's funny because when we met, she was the one who was lost, not sure what she wanted, working in this silly little café bookstore that I only kept going to because she was so intriguing. Every day I would go in and buy a paper from her. I'll admit I was first attracted to her looks—and her voice. She had this really sexy voice, and

I was drawn in by it. Every day I would ask how much the paper was just to hear her say "dollar fifty." Oh, that voice.

She sat behind the counter reading all these crazy books—I swear they were different every day. Everything from metaphysics textbooks to classic novels to political thrillers. And the music—that changed daily, too. Then one day she played B.B. King, and I saw my chance.

For two years, we had a great relationship. Again, the timing was so good. We were intensely in love with each other and with learning and with life. We fueled each other.

That belief is what made it impossible for me to stay with her after graduation. She inspired me to want so much out of life, to climb my mountain. And so I left.

The class began to settle into the lecture hall, and I watched Maggie perusing her notes. The first day in a large lecture class like this is the most important. It sets the tone and the respect level for the professor teaching the class. Maggie looked so poised, so in control, and—okay, I'll say it—so damn sexy standing up there. Oh how I wished I'd had a professor like that when I was in school.

She began to speak, and within minutes had mesmerized the class with her voice, her knowledge, her authority, and her passion. I watched

Maggie work the room—because that's what she did—and realized how much she had actually grown from when I knew her. I mean, I'd watched her lead her discussion sections, and I'd watched her finish her dissertation, but this was different. She'd matured. Flourished, even. If I'd had any qualms about leaving her, they were dashed when I saw how far she'd come. She would have been miserable in Tokyo while I ran around cities in Asia picking up leads for the wire service. The truth is I was miserable most of the time, and yet I knew it was something I had to do in order to move up in the world of journalism. I was paying my dues. How could I have inflicted that on Maggie?

Maggie never could—or, really, should—have dropped everything to go with me. Her work meant too much to her. You don't ask a person to give up their passion just to be with you. And, again, I had to be impressed with how much she had accomplished.

I'd kept up with her progress over the years and knew that her dissertation had been very well received, then she'd surprised them by turning the concepts in it into a mass market book that used telenovelas to illustrate the power structures in corporate communications. It was a great book—very funny and yet containing what many considered to be a break-through theory. She took a chance with it, though, as it was sure to upset the old guard of social scientists to write a commercial book instead of an academic one—heaven forbid you present an idea in an enjoyable way.

But it worked. The book was positively reviewed in some prominent business journals and made a lot of college course lists. Corporations and other universities were constantly inviting her to take a semester to be a visiting lecturer, but she hadn't left Berkeley except for some short speaking gigs here and there. Not yet. This was still her home.

As I watched Maggie lecture, I began to realize that I still wasn't sure where I wanted to be. Not yet. I'd spent three years building up a reputation as a good boots-on-the-ground journalist, but I wanted more. I wanted to be a good writer. I was tired of scrounging for bits of news and never signing an article. I wanted to really delve into stories and bring them to life and write about important issues. The wire service job had taught me a lot, but it wasn't enough anymore. I'd been back with Maggie for almost three weeks, and although I loved being with her, something was still missing. She was where she wanted to be, but I wasn't. Not yet.

I knew that I would be leaving the job at the wire service. I had taken all I could from the job, and it was time to move on. Maggie's belief in me would make it possible to keep climbing my mountain. Unfortunately, I knew that it would also mean leaving her again.

Ironic that the force that kept bringing me back to Maggie was also the force that fueled me to leave her. Her inspiration forced me to push myself to see what I was capable of and venture out into the world once again. When I had arrived in Berkeley, I was a burned-out workaholic sick of his job. Now I felt ready to tackle the world again.

I watched Maggie lecture and was filled with a profound feeling. Was it love? For me, love was such a complicated issue. It was more simple for Maggie, but I'd grown up in a house where love meant fights and divorce. I do know that Maggie conjured up feelings in me that I'd never felt for anyone else. What was it about her that brought about those feelings? Was it that she loved me while also giving me the freedom to find myself?

Looking at her, the glow on her face as she wrapped 300 snotty freshmen around her little finger, I had to hope that someday we would be at the same place at the same time again and could be together. That maybe someday love wouldn't be so complicated for me. That we could be in a world where we could live our passions while sharing our lives, but watching her lecture, I realized that now wasn't that time. She had found her life, but I still hadn't. I really did love her, but I also knew that I would have to leave her again.

Chapter Twenty-Two
CINDY

Mrs. Robert Billingsley V. Mrs. Biff Billingsley. Cindy Billingsley. The Billingsleys. Cindy and Biff Billingsley.

Okay, so I said yes. I mean, it's what I wanted, right? It's what I'd always wanted, right? I would be Biff's wife. Instead of deciding between a career or grad school, I would be Biff's wife. We'd get a cute little apartment in the city, and Biff would go off to his entry-level finance job every day. I'd get a job, too, but since I still had no idea what I wanted to do for a career—a degree in History meant I could do pretty much everything and nothing at the same time— it would probably just be temporary. I mean, Biff and I would start having babies in a few years so any thoughts of a real career might have to wait anyway.

My friends were really excited. They all screamed when I told them, and we started talking about dates and what colors my bridesmaids would wear and, naturally, who my bridesmaids would be. I knew I probably had to keep it to eight bridesmaids, and it would be so tough to choose just eight of my friends from the house. They all wanted to know who Biff's ushers would be—which frat guys he would pick—so they could figure out who they could scam on at the reception.

Naturally, Bunny would be my maid of honor. She was my best friend after all. Bunny didn't like the way she looked in pink, which was my first choice for bridesmaid dresses, so I told her she could help me pick them out. All in all, it was an exciting time. I was getting so much attention. I mean, it's what I wanted, right?

Things started to change when I started discussing the wedding with Biff's mother. Up until then it was kind of pretend, you know? Only then it was, like, real. Not that Biff's mom was mean to me. Actually, she really accepted me. She did. She kind of took me on as this pet project. We went to lunch at the Burlingame Country Club—very fancy schmancy. Waiters in suits served iced tea in these crystal glasses. I swear, though, the average age of the people there was, like 75. Like, were codgers the only members of the club or what?

I wore a cute sundress that Biff's mother said brought out the blue in my eyes. She wore a Chanel suit. I knew it was the real thing, too, you know? Biff's mother—Candace, she wanted me to call her, but it was kind of easier just thinking of her as Biff's mother—pulled out this little notebook and started discussing dates for the wedding.

She thought that a winter wedding might be nice, and I thought *Well, then pink would definitely be out*, and that we could have a formal reception at the country club—that, naturally, since the Billingsleys had been founding members, that would be the proper thing to do. I suppose it sounded nice, only I wondered if all the codgers would come, too.

Biff's mother said that she realized that my parents couldn't afford anything lavish and that Biff's father would be happy to help out and that, aside from using their name with the country club and paying for the reception, I should know that she was there for me whenever I had any questions.

She turned back to her notebook and began listing off everything we should have and how it should be done. I felt kind of overwhelmed and just kind of agreed to everything she said. When I went home later that night, Bunny said I shouldn't let her boss me around, but you know, he's her only son, and she did seem to know more about these things than I did.

I mean, I think you can see that everything was moving along, and I was getting everything I ever wanted. I was going to be a beautiful bride in a beautiful wedding with a beautiful husband. My future mother-in-law was being nice to me and helping me plan the wedding, and we'd have a beautiful life.

Only... why did it feel so claustrophobic? I started having these dreams where I was this bride only, I couldn't see the face of the guy I was marrying, so I didn't want to get married until I could see his face because I didn't want to spend my life with someone I didn't know. But I did know. I was marrying Biff, and I loved Biff, and he's all I ever wanted, right?

It's what I thought I wanted anyway. But then I started thinking about Biff's parents' living room. I know it sounds weird, but I remembered the first night that Biff and I spent together in his parents' house when they were away, and I noticed that they had one of those rooms that nobody ever goes into. It was beautiful and filled with antiques and stuff like that, and Biff's mother had a rope across it so nobody would sit in it. I swear I never saw anybody sit in that room. Even when they entertained, it was always outside on the patio or in the dining room, and maybe they did pass through the living room once, but I don't remember anybody ever sitting in there.

One day when I visited the house, I just stood and stared at that room. Everything was so pretty—so very very pretty but also so... dead.

I started looking at Biff's mother differently. When I first met her, I thought she was the prettiest woman I had ever seen. And so classy with her Chanel suits and perfect hair and perfect nails and perfect shoes. And so smart. She knew about everything: how to dress, what fork to use, how to walk so you don't fall over in high heels. I was always kind of afraid of her, though. I mean, she was so perfect. She never cracked, never really smiled. Her smooth skin was always so perfect, and I was always afraid of what she thought about me. I mean, I wasn't anything like her.

But now, now I saw her as kind of sad. That in a way, she was as lifeless as the furniture in her living room. I had this vision of her secretly going in and sitting in that living room by herself and enjoying all the things that her life had brought her. But they were just things. And they were dead things.

She was kind of lifeless, too. I remembered asking her once what she thought about an issue, like who she was going to vote for or something, and she said that she didn't really think about those things. And she didn't. She thought about the country club and the parties and the house but other than that… nada.

Bunny said she sounded like a Stepford Wife. I didn't know what she was talking about, so we found the original movie one weekend, and I swear it was all about Biff's family. I started having nightmares about Biff trying to remove my eyes and put them in a robot that looked like me and, I mean, I knew Biff wouldn't really do that. He loved me, didn't he?

I was so confused. I started wandering around campus. School had just started back up, and it was weird to see everybody going to classes when I wasn't. It was like they had a life there, but I didn't anymore. I really needed to talk to somebody. I felt weird going to the War Council because, after all, they'd helped me get Biff, so how could I tell them I wasn't sure I wanted him anymore?

I wandered over to Café Strada. Maybe there would be somebody to talk to there. There was: Kevin. Perfect. He'd understand. So, I sat with him at a table and spilled my guts. He didn't say a word, just looked at me with these big saucer eyes, and grinned like a lovesick puppy. I wondered if he was in love with some girl who wasn't giving him the time of day so I asked him, but he said he wasn't—just grinned at me. Well, he wasn't any help at all.

So, I went over to the I-House hoping I could catch Connor. I really needed a guy's perspective. He was in his room, so I told him what was bothering me. He gave me some speech about how life was like a rugby match, and you gotta play it through to the end. I didn't know what the fuck he was talking about. Then he tried to kiss me. He wasn't any help at all, so I left.

As I was leaving the I-House, I ran into Professor DeVillier and Coach Banks—I still called them that even though they kept telling me to call them Monique and Mike since I guess we were buds and all, but it still felt weird. Anyway, they said I looked troubled and did I want to join them for a drink. They said they were still interested in how I was doing even though I wasn't a War Council client anymore. Actually, they told me they'd left the War Council—weren't into it anymore. So, I took a chance that they would understand and sat with them at the I-House café.

I told them how I was confused. That here I was finally getting what I thought I wanted, but now I wasn't sure it was what I wanted because I didn't want Biff stealing my eyes and putting them in a robot that looked like me, but what else would I do because I couldn't work forever at the Edible Complex, and I couldn't go home to Santa Rosa because there was nothing for me there, so what was I going to do if I didn't marry Biff?

And Biff. I mean, what did I feel about Biff? He was still cute, even though he wasn't really as cute as he used to be, you know, since he, like, lost his ego. But he was still cute. Only he wasn't a big man on campus anymore; he was just an entry-level business dude who wore a suit and rode BART like every other entry-level business dude. His father had gotten him a job at some big finance firm, but they were one of those firms that had gotten in a lot of trouble because of insider trading and stuff so they weren't doing real well and couldn't pay him a lot. That was okay because Biff had a trust fund and everything, but still, he wasn't the same as he was in college. I kept trying to figure out if I really loved Biff or if I just loved the way he made me feel, you know?

Only now I kind of felt okay about myself without Biff, which is maybe why I was having dreams about faceless guys, you know?

Professor DeVillier and Coach Banks just kind of looked at me and nodded every once in a while. Then I noticed that they were holding hands. And they were looking at each other kinda funny and blushing every once in a while. Connor had kind of hinted something was going on between them. He'd say "Go Cal" and laugh hysterically. Like most of the things that came out of Connor's mouth, it made absolutely no sense to me, and I ignored him but then, then I noticed they were wearing wedding rings. What was this?

"Oh, well, we just got married."

"You what?"

"Yeah, it was a surprise to us, too. But it just seemed right."

"Yeah, we didn't even think about it."

"Yeah, we just did it."

"In Tahoe."

"Yeah, in Tahoe."

Then they giggled. Professor Hard Ass and the Coach giggled—I mean, like teenagers, you know? They smiled and looked into each other's eyes and I saw it. Oooo, gross. I mean, they were like, old, you know? Like way over 30 or maybe even 40. Shit, I didn't think people still thought about sex at that age, you know? But there it was: total lust.

After my initial revulsion at the image of them having sex washed away, I realized that they were really in love. That I was looking at what love was supposed to look like. I saw how you were supposed to look when you were ready to get married. I mean, Professor Hard Ass and Coach Banks? Can you think of anything so ludicrous? I couldn't, and yet it worked. They worked. They looked like they were meant to be together. I always thought I was meant to be with Biff, but I didn't look at him like that—like the way Prof was looking at Coach—anymore. Lately, Biff was kind of getting on my nerves if you want to know the truth.

And they said they didn't even think about it. They just did it. But I was thinking about it. I was thinking about it a lot. Maybe I shouldn't marry Biff, but then what was I supposed to do?

I was still confused when I got back to the apartment. Bunny was packing her stuff. She was supposed to be leaving to start law school at UCLA in a couple weeks—for some reason they always started like a month later than we did at Cal. We found a bottle of champagne in the refrigerator that was left over from a party and split it. Then we started making Kahlua milkshakes in the blender. We figured we didn't have a lot of gal time left and wanted to make it count.

After a while I noticed that Bunny seemed a little weird, so I asked her what was up.

"Oh, my parents."

"What about them?" Buster and Helen Merriman were these two very jolly rich types from San Marino, which is in Southern California near Pasadena, but I guess somehow more exclusive from the way they talked about it. I thought they were the coolest parents anyone could have.

"They said they think I should take a year off before law school and see the world."

"Wow." Shit, my parents didn't know the world extended past Santa Rosa.

"Yeah, they've offered me a European vacation if I defer law school a year."

"Bunny, I've never heard of parents telling—paying even—you not to go to school."

"Yeah, weird, huh? They're afraid I won't enjoy my youth, or that I'm rushing into law school before deciding it's what I really want and just want me to make sure."

"I swear, Bunny, your parents are the best."

"Naw."

"Yeah."

"Yeah? Well then why did they pull this on me now, three weeks before school starts? And who would I go with even if I did decide to go? I broke up with Barry last week, and you're getting married and…"

"You mean, you would take me to Europe?"

"Sure, Buster and Helen said they'd pay for me to take a friend. But like I said…"

"Well, maybe I can defer getting married for a year like you're deferring law school."

"You'd do that for me?"

"For my best friend in the whole world?"

"Best friend in the whole world!"

"Absolutamente."

"Let's do it!"

"Yeeeeee!"

We danced around the room. Actually, the room was beginning to dance around me. My head was spinning, and all I could think of was—yowza! Italian boys!!! I was going to see Italian boys! And maybe French boys! And Spanish boys! And I didn't have to marry Biff! I mean, I could figure out how I felt when I got back. If I came back. Maybe I'd move to L.A. and live with Bunny while she went to law school. Then I'd get to meet surfer boys! Whatever. I could think about it later. I wasn't going to be furniture. I wasn't going to be a Stepford Wife. This was so cool.

It just felt so great. Like a huge burden was lifted off my shoulders. I thought about how happy I was as I upchucked the Kahlua milkshake all over the bathroom floor.

Chapter Twenty-Three
MONIQUE

All right, I suppose people will make an issue out of the whole thing so I might as well address it now. Yes, we did it. Michael and I participated in that most bourgeois of all conventions: marriage. I did not take his name, but I am wearing a ring, and yes, we did get married. And it all came about because of one of Michael's—how should I say this—expressions of release.

Michael's exuberant "Go Cals" had been getting us into trouble for some time. Although we both fervently agreed that what we had between us was just physical and would burn out at some point, we couldn't seem to get enough of each other. And as we seemed to have a proclivity for enjoying each other's company in, well, unusual locations, the "Go Cal" vocalizations were heard by more than one confused passerby.

The problem was that, although we both recognized implicitly that our sexual voraciousness would burn out—I mean, we agreed it was just physical, and purely physical sex always burns out, correct?—it just wasn't burning out. If anything, it kept heating up. It was late in the summer when we hit upon a plan.

"A week away."

"A vacation."

"Wonderful idea."

"Sure fire."

We both astutely recognized that a week away, together, 24 hours a day, for seven days, would solve our dilemma. We were sure to make each other crazy. It was a brilliant plan.

Michael and I set off for Lake Tahoe in early August. It was one of the weeks between the end of summer school and the beginning of the fall semester and we both had time off. Michael had a friend who had a cabin by the lake that was available and would be the perfect setting for our brilliant plan.

The trip to Tahoe was relatively uneventful. The conversation was stimulating. As usual, Michael's comments either made me laugh or caused me great consternation. The man had a mind that I was unable to fathom, but I have to admit, I found it intriguing to try. At one point, Michael touched my thigh and the electricity forced us to pull off the road for a quick "Go Cal," but otherwise, as I mentioned, the trip was uneventful.

Upon arrival at the cabin, Michael and I were feeling the electricity once again—our normally voracious appetite perhaps galvanized by the realization that this trip meant we didn't have a lot of time left together. Michael kissed me and, as usual, I felt the surge associated with his touch. Why did this man bring about these feelings? What was it about this fireplug of a creature that excited and stimulated me like no one had before? The analytical impulses in my brain remained as perplexed as they were that first night in the War Council offices after our Kingfish escapade.

As usual, our connection was magnificent. Absolutely magnificent. I awaited the usual "Go Cal"—an event I'd grown quite fond of, I have to say—but this time, I was surprised to discover that it was not "Go Cal" that greeted my ears but a huge booming "Oh, Kiki, I love you so much I can't stand it."

MIKE

There, I'd said it. I had to say it. It had been in my noodle for weeks, rustling around in the ole brainola every painful moment that I wished to express my feelings to Kiki but didn't out of fear. Out of fear that she didn't feel the same. Out of fear that I'd spoil what we had. We had always said that it was just physical, and I was so damn afraid that that's all it was for her. But it came out.

I had to say it. I had to go for it—head for the try line, as they say in rugby—and I did.

I closed my eyes after my outburst, unable to look to see what reaction Kiki would give my admission. I mean, I'm not a weenie, but this was scarier than facing down a 200-pound tackler when you're carrying the ball.

"I love you, too, Michael."

What? Had I heard correctly?

"What?"

"I love you, too, Michael."

"Really?"

I opened my eyes. She was smiling and her face was so soft and her eyes so luminous and I was filled with such happiness I thought I was gonna burst.

Instead, I jumped up and started shouting:

"Oh my god! Oh my god! You love me? She loves me! Oh my god! I love you so much, Kiki. I never thought it would happen and it did and I love you and you love me and oh my god!"

I looked down and she was smiling but her eyes were all welled up and a tear came rolling down her cheek.

"Oh, Kiki, what's wrong?"

"Nothing. I'm just happy."

"Oh, Kiki."

I started kissing her all over her face and held her in my arms as tight as I could. It all just felt so damn good.

Kiki and I had a truly terrificola week together. We went hiking and swimming and spent long

239

hours just lying in each other's arms in the cabin. God, I loved this woman, every inch of her. I felt that, with her beside me, anything was possible. And then the realization hit me that I wanted this woman in my life… forever.

That night out at dinner I told her the story of Granny Banks. I knew where it would lead, but by then there was no stopping me.

Kiki sat across a table illuminated by candles and sipping her wine as I began my story.

"Granny Banks was my favorite person in the world. She was really there for me when my dad was acting like such a fart and cheating on mom. She thought he was acting like a fart, too, and he was her son. It kind of bonded us that this total freak was so closely related to us.

"I loved the house where Granny Banks lived. She lived only a few blocks away from us in Connecticut in this big old barn of a house. Granny Banks always felt that a house should be fun, and it was. There were tons of games and an outdoor jungle gym, and you could rough-house inside without worrying about breaking anything. Heck, Granny was a top roughhouser herself and was actually the one who taught me how to play rugby.

"My grandpa had died before I was born, so as long as I could remember Granny was alone—but she was one of those people who was never lonely. She had loved my grandpa, but more importantly, Granny Banks loved life. Loved everything about it. She was always

into something, some new hobby or project—
painting, theater, tennis, pickleball—she got a
master's degree in her late 50's and ran a mar-
athon at 65. She also always had tons of friends,
most of them half her age. I remember going to
her house for a dinner when I was in high school
and here was this 70-something-year-old woman
throwing a party for her friends who were all in
their 30s and 40s. They loved her and so did I.

"Six years ago, Granny almost died. She was
85 and came down with pneumonia, and they
didn't think she would make it. But she did. She
fooled them all and pulled through. And then
she did the impossible—she fell in love. She was
85 years old when she met Sam. Sam was a hospital volunteer, and they met while she was recu-
perating. Sam was a younger man—he was 82."

Kiki smiled and I continued.

"I remember the first time I saw Granny flirting
with Sam. That's what it was, too—unabashed
flirting. Granny just glowed and giggled and
twisted her hair around her finger while she
talked to him. Sam, being a dude, was showing
off by doing tricks with the magazine cart.

"After Granny left the hospital, they started
'courting' as she called it. I would visit and
she would be wearing her fanciest dress and
blushed when he rang the bell. Sam would call
on her with flowers and dressed in his best suit.
They looked like a couple leaving for the prom.
Five weeks later, they were married.

"I stood up for them at the service. If you can believe it, my dad—the fart—kept saying he thought they'd rushed into it. Can you believe that shit? I wanted to punch his lights out. 'Rushed into marriage.' Six months earlier, she'd been close to death, and he thinks they're rushing things.

"Anyway, Granny Banks and Sam had five really top-notch years together. Through them, I finally saw what love could be. They were thoughtful and considerate with one another. They would hold hands and make each other laugh and looked at each other with such admiration. Then, last year, a month from her 90th birthday, Granny Banks had a stroke and died."

Not that I'm a crier, but my eyes got a little funky, and my voice was starting to crack while talking about Granny Banks. I had never told anybody how much she meant to me before, and I guess it, you know, got to me a little. Kiki took my hand and smiled at me, her eyes welling up a little, too, as I finished my story.

"At her memorial service—which was packed full of Granny's eclectic menagerie of friends—Sam got up to speak. He talked about their courtship and how smitten he was the minute he saw Granny's smile. How he'd made up his mind on the spot that day in the hospital that he wanted this woman to be his bride and had set out to woo her and that their wedding day was the happiest day in his life. Sam said that they always knew they didn't have a lot of time together. Sam had a bad ticker and said that he always thought he'd go first, but it was Granny. Her death was quick and painless. Sam said she had lived life to its fullest and was loved and it was just her time to go. He said that we were the unlucky ones because we would miss her.

"And then Sam said something that really hit home. Sam said that because he and Granny knew they didn't have a lot of time together, every night before they fell asleep, they would hold hands and thank each other for another day together."

I looked over at Kiki, with her bloodshot eyes, red nose, and tears streaming down her face—god, she was beautiful. I held her hand a little tighter.

"And I guess why I'm telling you this, Kiki, is that I want you to know how grateful I am for the time we've had together, how much I love you, and that, well, I'd like to spend the rest of my life falling asleep holding your hand. So, um, how would you feel about marrying me?"

MONIQUE

With a proposal like that, how could I say no? Not that I wanted to. I was so in love with this man that I wanted to enjoy his embrace for the rest of my life. And yet he also made me want to conquer the world. With Michael at my side, I felt that anything was possible. So, we decided to get married—right away. Being in Nevada made that easy.

I felt it would be appropriate to conquer two of my fears at once. I've always been afraid of marriage—afraid of being trapped in the silently suffering martyrdom my mother placed herself in. I've also always been afraid of heights. Therefore, it was my suggestion that we get married atop one of the myriad mountains in the Tahoe area.

Michael loved the idea. I think he particularly appreciated the idea of tackling the convention of marriage in an unconventional way—kind of an ode to his grandmother, who sounded like a remarkable woman. We spent the day scurrying around trying to locate a mountain and a minister who would travel up a mountain to marry us.

Phenomenally enough, it all came together, and Michael and I were married at the peak of the Heavenly Valley ski area. Michael and I hiked up the mountain while the minister—a retired Anglican priest who preferred a tweed suit jacket and hat to the more traditional fleece garb you see around Tahoe—and his wife rode the lift. A skinny teenager helped the couple off the lift, and we all walked over to the peak, which had a gorgeous view of the lake below and of the hikers and mountain bikers on the trails around us.

Michael and I said our vows looking out over all of Lake Tahoe. I looked down the mountain and was not afraid. I said my vows and was not afraid. I looked into Michael's eyes, held onto his hands, and was not afraid.

Michael joined me as we stood before the minister, his wife, the lift operator, and the magnificent beauty of our surroundings and added to our vows the phrase: "With this person by my side, anything is possible."

Chapter Twenty-Four
MAGGIE

Suddenly, everything was crystal clear. I couldn't believe I hadn't seen it before. Ah, hindsight—everything is logical in hindsight.

I don't want you to think my epiphany came overnight because it didn't. Does it ever? Does anyone just go "poof" and see the light? I don't think so, or at least, it certainly had never happened that way with me. No light bulbs went off. No sunbeam shining through the clouds. More like a fog that slowly lifted until everything sparkled with such clarity. My insights came at the end of a long process of growth that began when I first fell in love more than six years ago.

I was alone. And yet, the wondrous thing about it was that I would never feel alone again.

It was October. Fall in Northern California. I walked around the Berkeley campus—my campus—reveling in my surroundings. I felt free and happy and secure. I delighted in everything around me: the academic buildings with their majestic bearing, the football games with their form and ritual, the students at Café Strada, so immersed in their studies and in each other. I loved my world, but mostly, I had finally come to love myself.

For the first time in my life, I realized that I really liked me. I liked my life. I loved teaching and learning and writing and my friends and my apartment. And, most importantly, it was a love that didn't come from a man or an accomplishment or any outside thing; it came from within and that could never be taken away. I was finally content in my own skin. Everything felt just so… so… clean.

Things were not so clean two months earlier. With the AWAC exposure, my breakup with Nick, my reunion with Bill, and the beginning of the fall semester, my life was in turmoil. It was messy. I hate messy. Messy is just, well, messy and confusing. I like clean—not in terms of lack of dirt but lack of clutter. I don't like a cluttered life. I like knowing where I stand and with whom and why—but I didn't know. There was Nick and there was Bill and there was me, and I was one confused chiquita.

Nick. I didn't know what to think about Nick. What was real, what was manipulation, what was love, what was psychological coercion? Who knew?

Bill. I didn't know what to think about Bill, the man who had helped me to believe in myself and believe in love, then left me without a backward glance and had let me down so many times with promised visits that never materialized.

This time Bill had kept his promise. He arrived on August 8th. He didn't ask me to meet him at the airport. Instead, he dropped his bags at a friend's house and showed up on my doorstep later that day. The sun was setting, and I hadn't heard from him all day—no call, no text, nothing. I had just about given up on him again when there he was casually sitting on the stoop reading a *New York Times*.

"Hi, Maggie," he said, lowering the paper to reveal himself, the totality that was Bill.

"Bill."

I was stunned. What should I do? I tried to take it all in. What did he look like? How did I feel? I wanted an on-the-spot monitoring of my feelings, and it just wasn't processing.

"You look great, Maggie."

He stood and kissed me on the cheek. Again, I tried to process it all, but it wasn't happening. How did he look? He looked like, well, Bill. But not Bill. This was weird.

"Uh huh. So, do you want to come inside?"

"Sure."

We went inside, and he began prowling around the apartment—the same apartment we had spent so much time together in three years ago.

"Wow, it looks the same. Well, not quite the same. You got some new prints, huh?"

Yep. I'll confess some of them I'd bought knowing he'd love them. "Uh huh."

"They look great. Wow, same view. Same couch. Remember this couch, Maggie?"

"It's my couch, Bill. I've seen it every day for three years." Uh oh. Too snippy?

"Yeah, sure, sorry. Stupid comment, huh?"

He looked at me. Oh god, don't do that. He looked just the same. A little older, a little worn out, maybe, but he had those same warm brown eyes, those pools I wanted to jump right into again. But I couldn't. I couldn't because I was so fucking scared of him ripping my heart out again.

"No, it's not stupid." I smiled and pulled myself away from those seductive eyes. "You want a drink?"

"Sure."

I needed a drink. I went into the kitchen and found a bottle of sauvignon blanc in the refrigerator. He followed me in and offered to open it for me. He brushed by me to get to the bottle opener, and I could feel my skin prickling as he went by. Damn physical chemistry. I didn't want to feel this, not now.

Bill handed me the filled glass. "To reunions."

I clinked my glass against his and drank. Downed it, I think you might say. We filled them again and moved into the living room and sat on the couch, our couch. We had spent hours on this couch talking about our dreams and our futures, and now we sat very stiffly just looking at one another. This was weird.

"You look so good, Maggie."

"Thanks."

"I've loved your emails and texts."

"Thanks."

"This is weird, huh?"

"Too weird."

"Yeah, I know. How do you feel, you know, about this? Us?" he asked, lowering his eyes as if fearing my response. I realized he was as nervous as I was.

"I don't know."

"Uh huh."

A moment of silence passed before I felt brave enough to ask: "How do you feel, Bill, you know, about this?"

He seemed please to get the chance to answer. "I feel like I've been waiting for this moment for so long and had so much to say, but now that I am looking at your beautiful eyes and your face and listening to your voice, all I can think about is kissing you." He laughed uncomfortably. "I guess it's a gut male response."

Another moment of silence.

"Well, what if I said I wouldn't mind a little gut male response?"

I mean, come on, I was thinking the same thing. The man was making me tingle all over. I had trouble looking him in the eye, but I just really wanted to see if the connection we had was still there.

Bill leaned over and kissed me, softly, tenderly, lingering. Then he scooted closer on the couch and took me in his arms and held me while he kissed me, softly, tenderly, lingering. And then I couldn't help myself, and I got into it. We got into it. Next thing I knew we were in my room going at it like people who haven't seen each other in, well, three years.

My visceral responses were feeling great, just great, while the rest of me—we're talking the brain and the heart here—couldn't feel a thing. It was so bizarre. Here I was with Bill, the man I had loved more than life itself, and he had finally come back, and I was numbed from any feeling whatsoever. It was bizarre.

I walked around the whole week in a fog like that. I was doing everyday chores, getting ready for the fall semester, things like that, and although I enjoyed being with Bill again, I had yet to feel anything.

Then one night I went back to the apartment, and he was cooking. He was standing in the kitchen in a t-shirt and briefs. Tomato sauce had splattered all over the stove and some had splashed his shirt. He looked up at me and smiled, sauce smeared across his face and said, "Mi amore, I am cooking for you. Do you want to hug me, the tomato sauce king of Berkeley?"

I don't know how to explain it except to say that the ridiculous sight of Bill standing in the kitchen in his underwear covered in sauce and grinning made me realize, for the first time since he'd returned, that he really did love me. Bill still loved me. I hadn't wanted to believe it. I'd been so numb I couldn't figure out what to believe. He'd been there for a week, had returned to me, and was physically right in front of me and living with me in my apartment, but I still couldn't feel it or see it.

But then somehow, there, with Bill looking just so ridiculous, I saw it. I saw love. That he loved me then and loved me now and that I wasn't wrong about what we'd had three years ago. That his leaving hadn't meant he didn't love me or that what we'd had wasn't special. I had equated his leaving with not really loving me, but there it was in black and white and red tomato sauce.

Bill really loved me.

I burst into tears. Not pretty little drops falling from my eyes but huge racking sobs that released all of the feelings I had been bottling up for a week—hell, for more than three years. I hadn't been wrong. I had loved him so much, and he had felt the same way. It was as if I was finally validated for believing in our love all those years. I had questioned everything when he left, and now I finally knew that it had been real.

I had loved and been loved and no matter what happened after this point, I could be solid in those feelings. I would never feel like a gutted fish again.

Bill came rushing over and held me in his arms as I laughed and cried and sobbed and blew my nose all over his shirt. Naturally, he had no idea what had set me off and thought maybe I'd been mugged or something. I told him I was just hormonal, and he seemed to buy it. He looked perplexed, but after I assured him I was fine, he returned to the stove.

I watched Bill as he stirred the sauce with his typical intensely focused attention. This man who had turned my life upside down loved me. But it still didn't explain why he'd left. Ironically enough, it was Nick who opened the door to that answer.

Nick, sweet Nick with the twinkling smile and loving eyes. Nick, who made me feel warm and comfortable and safe. Who taught me that I didn't need to be afraid of love. Nick. The thought of Nick brought a warm feeling to my insides and the memory of the two of us working our way through his music collection brought a delighted grin to my face. Unfortunately, while I was dealing with my feelings for Bill, there was no room for Nick. The clutter thing.

I tried to explain to Nick that it wasn't that I was still angry about the AWAC conspiracy. It wasn't that I didn't love him. I knew that what we'd had was real and not manufactured but this was something I had to do. At first, he wouldn't accept my explanation.

"I can't believe you just stopped loving me, Maggie."

"Don't say that, Nick. I do love you, but I have to do this. Besides, you're going to Paris."

"I would stay."

The way he looked at me, I knew he would. But it wouldn't be right.

"Don't you see, Nick? How can I ask you to give up one of your dreams?"

"But I don't want to go anymore."

"Come on, Nick. Don't do that. We had a wonderful relationship, and we may again. But now I think we both need a little space to clean things up. You with your adventures and your feelings about me and me with my feelings about you and about Bill. Maybe there will be a time when we can both have a clean slate and can be together without AWAC or Paris or Bill to clutter our thinking. If we're meant be, we will be. We'll be together."

"But we are meant to be together. Don't you see, Maggie?"

His pleading sounded familiar, as did my response.

"No, I don't. I wish I did, Nick, but I don't. Not now. Now with all that's happened and is happening. If I don't see things through with Bill, I will always wonder, and if you don't see things through with Paris, you will always wonder. If we don't let each other go and give ourselves the chance for a clean slate, we'll always wonder how much was the AWAC and how much was us. Don't you see, Nick? We need time to see if we really belong together."

"But I believe in us."

"I do, too, which is why I know we can handle being apart."

Our conversation had started outside my office, where Nick had surprised me with one of his patented chance encounters. It was dusk now as we crossed the quad. When we reached the Sproul fountain, the setting of our first date, Nick turned and hugged me tightly.

"I'm going to email and text you all sorts of pictures of berets and baguettes."

"I hope you will."

"God, I love you so much."

Nick and I just stood there in the twilight, holding onto each other and to all our spring and summer together had meant. It hurt to say goodbye, but it was a good hurt. A hurt that meant I'd felt—I'd felt love for this wonderful man who meant so much to me. I was letting him go, but I just knew that if it was meant to be, we would be together again.

It was a couple days before the words Nick and I had used in our goodbyes finally sank in, and it clicked as to whether I'd heard them before: Bill. They were the same words Bill and I had used three years earlier when he'd left. Only this time my role was reversed. Instead of believing so totally that I was right, now I was the one who needed time. I realized, and I know this may sound simple, that sometimes people do things that unfortunately hurt other people.

It doesn't mean they don't love those people or mean to hurt them: it just happens.

I returned to the apartment realizing that Bill's leaving was not an indictment of our love, just as my needing time was not an indictment of my love for Nick. Realizing that you can love someone while also choosing not to be with them liberated me. I had always linked loving someone to them being by your side. Now I realized that sometimes loving someone means letting them go. It was a good place to have gotten to because, as I returned to the apartment that evening, I was about to get the news that Bill was leaving again.

I had known for days that he would. When he first returned, it was to the safe secure environment that was our life in Berkeley. He was burned out on journalism—at least the form he'd been working—and life and he needed to refuel in a sense. At first, he reveled in the role of the happy hausfrau. He cooked, he followed me to lectures, went to museums and enjoyed the first breath of freedom he'd had since deciding to take his "time off" from the wire service.

But then I began to sense a listlessness growing in Bill. It wasn't me or even us but his life. It was like he was treading water. He wasn't moving forward. He was living in my life. I was happy in my life. I was fulfilled and growing every day. But he wasn't. He was still searching, and his searching would take him away from me.

I realized he would leave me again, but this time I wasn't afraid. I would be okay.

Bill left a month later. One of his Tokyo contacts was now an editor at *New York* magazine and offered him a reporter/researcher position. He was really excited because it offered the hope of moving up into a position where he could write the kind of long-form investigative pieces he'd always wanted to write. I was happy for him. Happy to see him excited and ready to tackle life again. I mean, let's face it: His hausfrau expertise was rather limited.

So, Bill and I said goodbye. He started to give me a speech about how much I'd meant to him and how hopefully we could be together someday, but I stopped him. I didn't need to hear it. Not this time. I knew. I had this image of us as these two old folks who find each other again and spend our days holding hands in the park. It made me feel good, as did the knowledge that our love would always be with us even if we were apart. I would always carry a part of him with me, and he would carry me with him. Our first breakup had left me with so many questions and now they were answered.

So, I was 31 now and I was alone. But the wondrous thing about it was I realized I would never really feel alone again. I had love. I had the love of two fascinating men, of life and who

I had become. That was something no one could take from me. Never again would I question that my feelings were real or that what I felt from others was real. And never again would I question the innate logic found within the mysterious workings of the world, which is of course why the War Council was such an atrocity and why I continued to argue its merits with Kathy at our weekly meeting at Café Strada.

"Sorry I'm late. I'll grab my latte and be right back," said Kathy as she dropped her bags and rushed toward the counter, waving to a depressing amount of coeds who'd used the War Council's services.

Naturally, I had forgiven Kathy for her part in the AWAC conspiracy. Funny how we give our friends so much more latitude than our lovers. Still, I couldn't understand why she was so obsessed with the War Council—or just "The Council" as she now liked to call it. I mean, come on, it was an experiment, an experiment that failed, in my opinion.

Kathy didn't agree. She was the only one of us to stay with the War Council and had managed to parlay an embarrassing little scandal with the chancellor into a national marketing ploy. She had hired new personnel, moved off campus, was beginning to turn a profit, and even had plans to start franchising the concept in other college towns across the country. It was crazy.

"What's so crazy about it?" Kathy asked as she sipped her latte.

"Everything."

"Everything what?"

She was getting that smug Kathy look that she knew made me crazy.

"Kathy, you can't try to control relationships the same way you can't control, I don't know, the weather. You just go with it."

"Go with it how?"

"Go with what how?"

"Go with the weather how?"

"What do you mean?"

"How is it you learn to go with the weather, Maggie?"

"Sheesh, Kathy, I don't know. I guess you learn that when it rains, you should wear a slicker, and when it's sunny, you wear a hat."

"Uh huh. Relationships as weather. Interesting concept, Maggie. New book?"

You can see how patronizing she could be, right?

"Don't get like that, Kathy."

"Like what?"

"You get defensive when I disagree with you."

"I'm not defensive. Go ahead. Make your point."

The woman could be exasperating.

"I'm just saying that you can't coerce the weather to be like you want just like you can't coerce people to be like you want. All you can do is go with what you're given and make the best of it or learn from it."

"I see your point, Maggie, but I don't see us as trying to coerce anything. I see us as supporting people through the minefield that love has become."

"Putting electrodes in a man's chair?"

"Sometimes people need a little shove in the right direction."

"But that's just it. Who are you to decide what the right direction is?"

"So, we should have left the guy sitting in front of the TV the rest of his life while his wife became more and more resentful, and their marriage fell apart?"

"You could have supported her without the electrodes."

"Maggie, we don't have the time. We have to get quick results and move on. There are a lot of people to help out there. The electrodes worked. Period."

"What about our first client, what was her name, Cindy? We coerced her boyfriend—okay he was a prick but that's beside the point—into proposing because that's what she said she wanted, and then she runs off to Italy with her friend."

"That breakup would have occurred sooner or later. We probably just saved that poor girl two or three miserable years. He would have dumped her, and she would have been left with no self-esteem AND no boyfriend. This way Cindy realized all she had apart from Biff and is embarking on a brand new life as we speak."

Kathy finished by taking a slurp from her latte and looking rather pleased with her explanation. I was incredulous.

"How do we know that?"

"What?"

"This little scenario you've concocted to relieve yourself of guilt."

"I have no guilt."

"Still, how do we know what would have happened? We stuck our noses where they didn't belong—and I take full responsibility for my part in that—and sent her life off on a course it never would have taken otherwise."

"I don't agree," said Kathy. "Her life took that path, which means it was the path she was meant to take. We tried to intervene, but she still headed off in the direction she was meant to."

"Which means we never should have intervened."

"Which means it only helped for us to intervene."

What the...? I had to ask: "When did you get like this?"

"Like what?"

"Like into playing god."

"I'm not playing god. I'm helping people who desperately need the support. I'm part of a team helping people who desperately need it. You were right, Maggie. I was wrong and you were right. It's a war out there. People have forgotten how to act on the battlefield that is love and I, we, are now there to help them."

I felt like I was looking at a stranger. Love as a battlefield? If I'd learned anything, it was that love was a miraculously wondrous mystery, so why was Kathy overanalyzing it so much? Why was the world overanalyzing it so much? I mean, I had to admit the War Council was successful, but it was just so wrong. It seemed I'd created a monster.

I was never going to win the argument with Kathy while she was in the mood she was in, so I left her handing a business card to a lovelorn guy whose girlfriend had apparently just ditched him and wandered back to my office. I refused to buy into Kathy's solution of coercing the world to be a certain way. It just left out so many unexplored avenues.

As you can probably tell, the past year had really changed me. Instead of trying to control my world and see only one path as the right path, I was reveling in how many directions were open to me. What had happened with Bill, with Nick, and even the stupid War Council had brought me to this place where I could just enjoy my life and where it was taking me. I had let both the men I loved go. Fate would bring me together with one of them… or someone new. I really felt that ultimately I was going to end up with whoever or whatever was right for me and felt so open to what the future might bring.

I began to see how the world seemed to run on this invisible course that sends us signals to help guide us on our journey if we're open to accepting them. I wasn't able to see them before, but now I did, and life for me had become a wonderful adventure filled with possibilities. I was ready to move on armed with the knowledge that whatever path I chose would be the right one because I chose it.

I was still musing about the wondrous nature of the universe and its signals when I arrived at the departmental office to pick up my mail. Blanche, the communications department office manager, was on the phone when I walked in but gestured wildly for me to wait and talk to her.

"Maggie Maggie Maggie," Blanche admonished as she hung up the phone.

"What?"

"You haven't given us your answer as to where you're going next year so we can start making plans."

Going? What was she talking about? Then I remembered: my sabbatical. I had been corresponding with a number of programs and organizations that wanted me to come and lecture on my book, but par for the course in the university system, the prospectus had been sent to my department chair so long ago that I'd forgotten all about it. I'd practically forgotten I was taking a sabbatical.

"Did Lazarus get back with his recommendations?"

"Yes, he left them on my desk this morning. Dr. Lazarus suggests that you might look at the offers to lecture at either the Annenberg School of Communications at NYU or the American University in Paris."

It took a while to sink in.

"New York or Paris?" I said, a huge grin breaking out on my face.

"Yeah, toughie, huh?"

New York or Paris. I felt a little lightheaded and started to giggle. Blanche looked at me like I was mad. I left the office and started down the hall, my head spinning at the possibilities. I was being asked to make a choice and the world was not particularly shy about giving me a sign.

New York Paris. Paris New York. Nick Bill. Bill Nick. Or Berkeley. It was my sabbatical. I could do whatever I wanted.

I thought about my options, and as I stepped out onto the quad with the sun streaming through a crack in the clouds, the leaves on the trees rustling in the breeze and the faint sound of voices cheering "Go Cal" in the distance, I knew what my decision would be. I knew where I belonged.

It was just so logical.

THE END

About the Author

In her 20+ years as a writer and editor, Ann Shepphird has covered everything from travel and sports to gardening and food to design and transportation for a variety of publications.

Now Ann is tackling her favorite topics—rom-coms and cozy mysteries—for 4 Horsemen Publications. The University Chronicles series of rom-coms are based on Ann's days as a college-level communications instructor, while the Destination Murder mysteries combine Ann's experiences as a travel journalist with her stint working for a private investigator.

Ann lives in Santa Monica, California, with her long-time partner, Jeff, and their furry companions Melody and Winnie. When she's not writing, Ann is most likely to be found on a tennis court or in her garden.

Discover More...

annshepphird.com

facebook.com/authorannshepphird

Instagram: @ashepphird

Twitter: @ashepphird

ashepphird@gmail.com

Books...

Destination: Maui,
a Destination Murder Mystery

Destination: Monterey,
a Destination Murder Mystery

4 Horsemen Publications

Romance

Emily Bunney
All or Nothing
All the Way
All Night Long
All She Needs
Having it All
All at Once
All Together
All for Her

Lynn Chantale
The Baker's Touch
Blind Secrets

Mimi Francis
Private Lives
Second Chances
Run Away Home
The Professor

4HorsemenPublications.com

CPSIA information can be obtained
at www.ICGtesting.com
Printed in the USA
BVHW081005250821
615124BV00006B/269